Fill Your Own Cup

A Sweet, Contemporary Romance Fiction About Women's Empowerment and Chasing Your Dreams

Copyright © MADISON BUCKLEY

All rights reserved. No part of this publication may be reproduced, distributed, or transmitted in any form or by any means, including photocopying, recording, or other electronic or mechanical methods, without the prior written permission of the publisher, except in the case of brief quotations embodied in critical reviews and certain other noncommercial uses permitted by copyright law.

Table of Contents

ONE	1
TWO	13
THREE	23
FOUR	33
FIVE	50
SIX	59
SEVEN	66
EIGHT	77
NINE	86
TEN	97
ELEVEN	105
TWELVE	112
THIRTEEN	131
FOURTEEN	143
FIFTEEN	153
SIXTEEN	168
SEVENTEEN	184
EIGHTEEN	199
NINETEEN	208
TWENTY	215
TWENTY-ONE	225
TWENTY-TWO	236
EPILOGUE	243

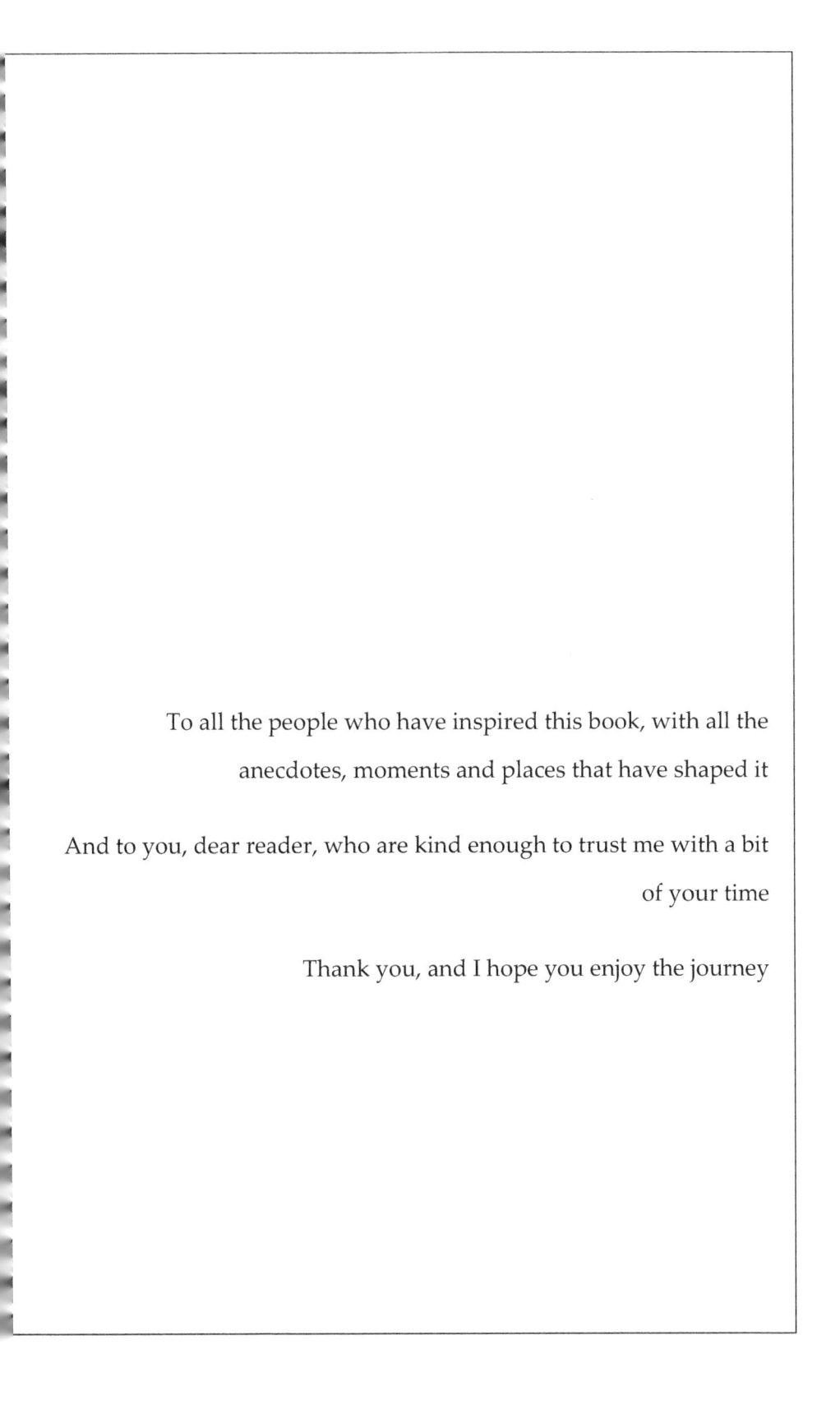

To all the people who have inspired this book, with all the anecdotes, moments and places that have shaped it

And to you, dear reader, who are kind enough to trust me with a bit of your time

Thank you, and I hope you enjoy the journey

ONE

I have to admit, when I left my student job as a bartender in my last year of uni in Nottingham, I didn't think I'd ever find myself working behind a counter again. But life has a funny way of frothing up unexpected surprises, I suppose.

So here I am, thirty-two years old, accidental barista extraordinaire serving up lattes and the occasional iced mocha at a little café on Bermondsey Street in London. Okay, maybe "extraordinaire" is a bit of a stretch, but I can make half-decent foam hearts and I can name at least four ways to brew coffee now. So.

As I step into White Cuppa House for my morning shift just a couple minutes past eight, a wave of familiar scents wraps around me like a cosy blanket. The air is infused with the aroma of freshly ground coffee, mingling with the sweet fragrance of warm pastries just out of the oven.

"Good morning sunshine!" Charlotte's voice rings out as I walk in, her apron already tied in a neat bow and her hands filled with a tray of *pains au chocolat* and croissants she's just collected from our little kitchen. I join her behind the counter and grab my own apron hanging from the wall.

"Morning, beautiful. Sorry I'm late—I'll sort these out," I say pointing at the tray of *viennoiseries* she just laid down on the counter. "What did I miss?"

"Oh, you're grand—it's still quiet for now, I've only served two flat whites and an English breakfast. Nothing too exciting." She lowers her voice. "But Lucia came here on a date yesterday with an absolute hottie and they seemed to reaaaaally get along."

Charlotte is a bundle of energy, her natural enthusiasm radiating from every pore at any hour of any day. She has beautiful hazel eyes, though they're often hidden beneath a fringe of thick, mahogany curls that frame her lively face. With a contagious laugh and a singing accent that can brighten even the gloomiest of days, her dimples deepen when she smiles. Her white Irish skin seems to glow with natural warmth, and her rosy cheeks are perpetually flushed with excitement. She has a petite frame, but her confidence makes her an innate leader, and I have seen her wrap many difficult customers around her fingers and turn them into loyal regulars over time.

She also likes a good gossip, which I have to admit, I do too.

"How is it that all the fun always happens when I'm not working?" I complain, grabbing a pair of tongs to place the pastries in our display, next to the cakes and muffins Charlotte already laid out before I arrived.

"I know, right? And it's not fun for me either, having to keep it to myself until I see you again. It's not exactly as if I could share it with Cassandra, is it?" I try to picture Cassandra, our other colleague, entertaining a light-hearted, gossipy conversation with Charlotte. I can't. Come to think of it, I don't even remember hearing Cassandra do small talk. Ever. "Anyway, I'm dying to know how they got on after they left, I hope she'll stop by at lunch."

I nod vigorously as I finish displaying the last croissant and head to the kitchen to grab the tray of our savoury offerings.

The familiar faces of our regulars begin to trickle in, and the café comes alive with conversations and the clinking of cups, welcoming and warm in the morning sun of a beautiful spring day. Vintage teacups, delicate china plates, and sepia-toned photographs decorate the walls, remembering Bermondsey Street just the way it was when the café opened, some sixty years ago. The furniture, a mix of mismatched chairs and quaint wooden tables, invites our patrons to settle in and stay a while. At this hour of the day, however, most of our clients are hurried commuters eager to grab their morning fix of coffee to sip on their way to their nine-to-five jobs in the city—as I used to do.

"Here you go, skinny cappuccino with extra shot," I announce a moment later, handing Mrs Tucker her reusable thermos cup.

Up until nine months ago, I was a motion designer at Banders, an independent experiential marketing agency, breathing life into pixels and making animated magic. But as recession hit the UK after Brexit, the pandemic and all the shenanigans the past few years have brought about, Banders was sold to a bigger company, and I was made redundant after two and a half years of service. Redundant, like that extra shot of espresso Mrs Tucker requests be added to her cup every morning, although her jittery hands and bloodshot eyes tell me she's already brimming with caffeine.

After three months of applying to every motion designer job under the sun, I resolved to take on this part-time job at my local café to make ends meet while I plan my next career move. In the six months I've been working here, this charming café has become my sanctuary. I've brewed countless cups, sampled all the bakery items on the counter (the gluten-free banana cake is heavenly) and slowed the alarming haemorrhage from my savings account—thank God.

But more importantly, I have met Charlotte, who turned from colleague to friend almost instantly. And although it's only been a few months, I couldn't imagine my life without her now. Together, we've bonded over spilled espressos, started off our caffeine-craving regular customers' day on the right foot, and shared long, nice chats, deep and light, during quiet hours behind the counter.

I suppose it's not that unusual—I got along rather well with my co-workers at Banders, and had even grown quite close to some of them. When I left the company, we promised to stay in touch, but as weeks and months drew by, no one reached out and connections just kind of died out. Apart from Debbie, of course, whom I text with every so often but haven't seen in a while. I make a mental note to send her a message and suggest a catch-up.

As the morning frenzy calms down, the café takes on a warm, cosy glow, and the air fills with a simmering chatter. In the afternoon, couples find refuge in corners, stealing kisses between sips of cappuccino (no sign of Lucia or her mysterious man today), while friends gather around tables, swapping stories while sharing a slice of lemon drizzle cake.

There's something magical about this place, an energy that draws people in and wraps them in a caffeinated embrace. And with our regulars, White Cuppa House feels like a real community, where people come and go, but eventually always come back. Charlotte and I get glimpses of everyone's lives, and share a smile and a few words with them. Like Juliette, the middle-age French lady who works at the charity shop ten numbers down the street. Or Hugo, our handsome regular with a penchant for americanos.

"Another successful day in wonderland," I remark, undoing my apron and packing a leftover sandwich to take home as my day-long shift comes to a close. "Worlds apart from the day I'll be squandering tomorrow browsing depressing job boards on my computer."

Charlotte winces, her hands flying deftly as she expertly crafts a beautiful latte art design. "Sounds fuuun. Are you sure it's worth it? Why look for another gig when you could be spending all your days working away with *moi* at the café, spreading happiness, one cup at a time?"

I smile. "When you put it like that... Hey, maybe I'll bring my laptop down in the afternoon and work from here for a couple of hours. That way I can search for jobs and we can keep each other company, how about that?"

"Deal." She nods. "And if you play your cards right, there might even be free coffee."

I giggle and give her a friendly hug goodbye before stepping outside. Away from the milk steamer and boiling kettles, I shiver a little bit in the chilly late afternoon and pick up my pace striding down the street.

My flat is only a short walk and three flights of stairs from White Cuppa House. This is rather convenient for someone clumsy like me, because it means I can run home and change clothes if I spill coffee all over myself thirty minutes into my shift. Not that it happens very often, but you know. It did, and probably will again.

I hang up my jacket, kick off my shoes and drop into the welcoming cushions of my sofa with a groan of contentment. I take a mouthful of the sandwich I packed, and fall into a blissful silence as I munch away my dinner.

My legs and back are killing me after a full day at the café, and for a second I bask in the idea of a warm bath to relax my sore body. Is this what it feels like to get old? I understand an increasingly sedentary lifestyle is the killer of our generation, but right now, this doesn't sound too bad to me.

I don't know how Charlotte does it every day. As much as I love working with her, I can't bring myself to take the plunge and commit to a full-time barista career. And it's not just because I feel old beyond my years—working away at a little café day in and day out is just not where I pictured myself. I still come home at night with the same dreams and the same passion for the film industry that have been guiding me since the internship I did in my first year of uni. And in any case, I won't become a head of coffee anytime soon, and, in the meantime, my meagre salary as a part-time barista barely covers the rent for my one-bed flat.

I love my flat. It isn't big, but having a whole place to yourself in the centre of London is a luxury few single people my age can afford.

I still remember the first time I visited it. It only took me one quick look at it to feel this was exactly where I belonged, and I'm so grateful that through the tumultuous months I've had, it has remained my safe space. In the three years I've been nesting here, the living room is where I've passed most of my time unwinding, chatting with guests or working away on my laptop. It is intimate and inviting, with soft, earthy tones and a few houseplants, creating a soothing atmosphere. Like a warm hug after a long day. My plush, toffee-coloured sofa takes centre stage, adorned with an assortment of throw pillows in muted shades of blues and greens. The worn-in cushions hold the imprint of countless cosy nights spent sharing a bottle of wine with a friend, curled up with a good book or lost in captivating conversations.

As the sun starts to set, I grab a match box from the small drawer of the wooden coffee table to light up a scented candle, and switch on my vintage-inspired floor lamp. It casts a gentle light that dances around the room to the sound of the crackling wood wick, bathing the walls in a warm glow. I haven't set up a proper dining area, so I usually just eat from the coffee table, watching something on my laptop or peering out of the window, observing the world pass by.

It's here, in the cosy nook I've created for myself, that I continue my creative pursuits.

I started my own podcast as a hobby and a way to stay connected with friends and colleagues during the pandemic, and I have kept it up semi-regularly ever since. I try to post an episode every other week or so, depending on my schedule and my guests' availability. They are often women I meet out and about in London, every now and again a listener suggests a woman in their circle that has a great life story and I should invite on the podcast. It takes a bit more time to organise but it's always been worth it. I do the sound editing myself, so I still have to spend a quite a bit of time after each interview before the podcast episode is ready to come out, but it's been an enjoyable side hustle.

I switch on my computer and open the editing software, excited as I recall the conversation I had with my guest just a few nights ago. This episode's guest is Laura, a transgender woman that I met at the gym one day. I complimented her on the definition of the muscles in her back, and we became friendly. She told me her transition journey and I almost *begged* her to come share her story on Ellie's Track.

I love that the little amateur podcast I started in my living room a couple years ago has created a space for cis and trans women alike to share their memoirs, their struggles, and their triumphs. I hit the play button and revisit our conversation, my smile growing wider as I remember everything we discussed and just how organic it felt. Laura's words are powerful, and as she recounted her journey, her resilience and determination captivated me. For over an hour, we talked about self-discovery, failed dating, and the beauty of embracing one's true self.

From the beginning I naturally gravitated towards female speakers, and except for one non-binary person, all my guests have been extraordinary, strong women, with unique life paths and hilarious anecdotes to tell. My personal favourite to date has to be this tiny old lady called Mariam that I met at an awards ceremony once when I still worked at Banders. She was sat next to me at the dinner table, and I spent the whole evening listening to the incredible stories of her time working as an animal care worker in a wildlife sanctuary in South Africa.

I have loved diving into fascinating conversations with them, talking about their lives, their backgrounds, their experiences, and the lessons they've learned along the way. I have released just short of 30 episodes now, and some of them have been getting a lot of attention and comments from listeners. I wasn't expecting this interest at all when I started, but now it keeps me motivated to persevere.

I make a few initial cuts and minor sound edits, but to be honest, the raw take is already pretty good. Laura is a natural, and I have noticed the episodes that are the most commented on are often the least reworked ones.

I send a text to Laura to tell her I'll finish the edits and should be able to send her the final cut tomorrow so that she can approve it before I post the episode.

I open Netflix and prepare for an evening of *pretending-to-watch-a-show-while-endlessly-scrolling-through-nstagram* when my phone pings with Laura's reply: "*Brilliant! Thank you, Ellie. Jack has been nagging me to know when it'll be ready so she can send it to his friends and tell them his missus is famous. No pressure! Haha.*"

I smile to myself, remembering Laura's mellow face and soft voice whenever she mentioned her boyfriend Jack. This just serves as another reminder that despite the challenges life throws our way (whether it's grappling with a wrong gender assignment at birth or, albeit less dramatic yet still immensely frustrating, being made redundant), the journey ultimately leads us to our true passions and to the people who make our existence more meaningful.

As for me, this journey is a delicate balance, not entirely what I initially expected, and hopefully just a stepping stone to greater accomplishments on the horizon. But for now, I must admit, it's not too shabby at all.

TWO

"Dan, watch out!"

A mix of cheers and jeers of spectators fill the air as Dan dives for the ball coming his way and misses it by an inch, landing heavily in the sand as the opposite team scores yet again.

The sun is shining, the ground warm beneath my feet, and our weekly volleyball game is in full swing at Southwark Park. It is HOT. Hot and clammy. And my team is losing.

We are down one player, which means the other squad can swap out people more often than us and have more chance to recover, and it shows. There is some heavy breathing going on here, and not the sexy kind. The SPF I applied an hour ago isn't doing much for my pale skin, and countless strands of hair have escaped from my once neat and tight braids, leaving me looking rather dishevelled. And I will spare you the details, but let me just say this: chaffing. Eek.

Dan grunts and scrambles off the ground, rubbing the sand off his hands and knees. He shrugs it off as he picks up the ball, trying to play it cool, while Amar couldn't appear smugger than he does right now. He is on the opposite team today, and he's a great competitor, which doesn't help.

"What's that, twenty to twelve?" he asks innocently.

"*No,*" Dan replies, annoyance clearly hinting in his voice, "that's eighteen to twelve, and it's only the first set so don't get too excited. We can still—"

"I reckon we should check with the refs", Amar continues, pretending not to hear him. "Charlotte! What's the score?" he calls to her. Dan jolts his head impatiently and poor Charlotte, who was minding her business a minute ago, now looks on high alert and as if she's just been punched in the gut.

"I-I think it's twenty to…"

"Okay okayyyy, let's move on!" I cut over her, and I can almost sense her relief and I *see* her shoulders relax as I defuse this simmering male ego conflict between our guys. I know Amar is just being playful, but I'm not sure Dan will respond well to much more taunting. I nudge him to serve the ball, which he does with a bit more force than necessary, and thankfully, Amar falls quiet and swiftly goes back to his mark on the other side of the net to catch it.

Contrary to Dan, he has an exquisite sense of humour, great conversation and I really enjoy his company. And yes, I very much prefer him being on my team than playing against him, because the alternative means a lot of diving in the sand and not much chance at winning.

When the gloomy winter days finally started to get warmer and it became pleasurable to spend extended periods of time outside, I decided to look for an outdoor activity. I wanted to mix things up from the gym a bit and hopefully meet more people, too. I always wanted to master the art of roller-skating and maybe join the cool teenagers skating their way along Southbank, blasting music and doing complex figures on ramps at the skate park under the arches by Waterloo Bridge. So I looked up local group sessions and took my brand new skates, my full-body protective gear and my unwavering optimism to a taster class in Southwark Park on a Saturday afternoon.

It did not go well.

I mean, if I had known that we would spend the whole hour learning how to fall and stand back up (one of the two, as it turns out, I'm really good at), I would probably have thought twice about it. After sixty long, painful minutes, I felt like the only taste of roller-skating I got was that of utter embarrassment and a lot of London dust.

In a feeble attempt to lift my spirits, I grabbed myself a cookie and a cappuccino from the coffee truck in the park and took a little stroll, incredibly aware and grateful for the steadiness of my steps in my trainers. As I was contemplating my miserable failure at roller-skating and the questionable life choices I make (not to be dramatic), my feet carried me to the volleyball pitch where the game was already in full swing, and I stopped to watch the guys play as I ate my snack.

Amar was the first one to notice me peering at them, and he invited me to join his team as they were one player down—or so he said. I instantly loved his energy and warmth, and I was looking to meet people after all, so I took him up on the offer and joined in. I had so much fun, and was pleasantly surprised at my performance… although, in hindsight, it was probably a good mix of beginner's luck and an extra ego-boost under Amar's praises.

And I mean, he does have a certain charm. He is tall and athletic, his lean muscular build a testimony of many years spent playing all sorts of sports. His warm, sun-kissed complexion hints at his Middle Eastern roots, much like his traditional, occasionally somewhat old-fashioned values but never in a way that made me feel uncomfortable. He has a genuinely kind and laid-back nature, as I quickly came to realise, and a presence that I could easily be drawn to.

Yet there's something missing, that level of chemistry that makes you weak in the knees and sends an electric shock up your spine. We've hung out a couple times outside the pitch, just the two of us, and even exchanged a timid kiss at the end of the night, once—but I didn't feel the spark. Nope, all I'm getting is a lukewarm latte vibe. And no one likes a lukewarm latte.

Still, no matter how many times I have then turned down his attempts at going out again, and even after I told him exactly how I felt about us, his enthusiasm can't be tamed, and he's kept trying. You got to give it to him, the man knows how to chase a woman.

And yes, sure, it's nice to get the attention, but I think my heart is still recovering from my short-lived romance with Elliott; my ex. We had something promising going on, or so I thought. We even spent a weekend getaway together in Cambridge—it was quite romantic, actually. But then, instead of progressing further, things started to feel a bit odd, as if he was pulling away. When I asked him about it, Elliott confessed that he felt as if he wasn't falling in love with me, and didn't want to lead me on. Which, let's be honest, seemed too little, too little too late after six months, but there you go.

Men.

So anyway, the last thing I want is to put Amar through the same thing and get myself into another situationship that will end in disappointment. Besides, I have dreams to chase and bills to pay, so I should really focus on finding a new job right now. Love can wait.

As the game resumes, Charlotte's cheering from the sidelines grow louder, like her life depends on it. We could really have done with an extra member in the team today, but she did a leg session at the gym this morning and assured us that she'd be a burden rather than an asset, so she passed on the game and resolved to cheer us on instead. I do have to say, I feel a little bit insulted to hear so many "Go Dan!" and nowhere near as many "Go Ellie!" when *I'm* the one doing most of the saves. But I suppose my Libra ego can handle the perspective of a defeat a lot better than Mr Capricorn over there (Charlotte likes to keep tabs of everyone's star signs and she *will* give you your full birth chart if she manages to get your birthplace and time of birth out of you).

After what feels like an eternity of lunging and squatting, Amar's team predictably win the first set and we take a short break in the game. Charlotte trots over, handing me a towel and some water.

"You're spiking it like a pro out there!" she says. "Proper cannonballs."

"Thanks! It's nice to hear *some* words of encouragement at last," I say grudgingly, passing her back the bottle of water after taking a few big gulps out of it.

I wipe the sweat off my face and tug at the rubber bands holding whatever is left from my braids, releasing the last strands of hair from them. I duck my head, running my dusty fingers through my already sticky mane. As I rise again, shaking my loose hair off, I can see Charlotte is peering over to Dan who is downing a bottle of Lucozade.

"You should have played with us," I add, as her gaze comes back to me. I turn around, pointing at the back of my head, and she takes the hint and parts my lock into two even sections before starting to braid it. "You could have helped us win and Dan would be in a better mood, and—"

"Trust me, you'd still be losing," she counters, unapologetically. "I know a lost cause when I see one, and there's no way your team is winning today, Ellie. Just accept it. Hair band."

Fair.

"How are things between you and Amar, though?" she asks as she tugs at the rest of my hair.

"Well, you know the whole story already," I shrug. "Nothing's changed, really. We've hung out a couple times, had some laughs, but I'm just not feeling it." She gives my shoulder a soft pat and I hand her the second band. "He's a great guy, but maybe just not the one for me. Or maybe it's not the right time. I don't know. Either way, I'm just focused on sorting my life out right now, so I don't think I can get involved with anyone at the moment. You know, unless it's Jason Momoa or something—then I could be convinced."

I turn around to face her again and she gives me a knowing nod, her expression filled with understanding.

"Girl, I hear you. Sometimes, you have to take a break from dating and prioritise yourself. Fill your own cup first, and when the time is right, somebody will walk into your life and sweep you off your feet and carry you into the sunset."

I roll my eyes at the drama in her words but grant her a grateful smile, have another sip of water and head back to my team.

As the game continues, I channel my inner sports goddess, spiking, serving, ploughing through the fatigue and the heat, and we manage to score the first three points in the set. Charlotte resumes her relentless cheers and thankfully there are no more signs of the previous tension between the boys. Between serves, I steal a glance at Amar, and smile fondly at the frown of concentration on his face as he lunges forward to catch the ball. He really does deserve someone great, somebody who'll appreciate him for all he is and will be crazy about him, but I don't think that someone could turn out to be me.

Laughter fills the air, a small group of strangers having joined Charlotte and others on the sidelines to watch our set and cheer us on. Here on the court, with my bare feet on the sand, my heart is content. For the time that our games last, I don't feel the usual nagging anxiety in my stomach or the worried thoughts in the back of my head. I let the endorphins engulf me and adrenaline move my body until it is positively exhausted.

This is my happy place, and nothing can disrupt this feeling of contentment.

Charlotte applauds loudly as Amar misses the ball by two inches and Dan, who spiked the scoring ball, looks extremely pleased with himself.

"Nice try, Amar, but you'll have to work harder to beat us!" I call out facetiously.

"Excuse me, have we been playing in parallel universes this whole time?" he shoots back in disbelief. My sass and audacity pay off, though, because the next second, he misses another ball that lands just at his feet, greeted by a mix of cheers and boos from the sidelines. "Don't kick a man when he's down, guys!"

As the sun sets and the game draws to a close, we gather in a huddle, sweaty, some of us victorious, and all desperate for a cold drink. We leave the court and make way to the Raven's Roost, our local pub. Amar, walking alongside me, wipes the perspiration off his forehead with the back of his hand.

"So, Ellie, what are your plans for the rest of the day?" he enquires.

"A long bath and a lie-in. And a takeaway pizza. In no particular order."

"A little room for me?"

I jab his shoulder. "Sorry, it's a one-person-only kind of deal. And I wouldn't let anyone between me and my pepperoni pizza."

"It was worth a try," Amar says with a shrug, opening the door for me as we reach the entrance of the pub. "But the offer stands. If you change your mind, you have my number."

"Thanks," I reply as I step inside. "I'll keep that in mind. Does your offer extend to a large glass of iced tea? Because I am parched."

THREE

Most days, White Cuppa House is a tranquil coffee haven, an enjoyable stop for London commuters and local passers-by. The skilled baristas (that includes me) work together behind the counter, serving up hundreds of steaming cups from the early hours in the morning until the late afternoon.

Today, however, is not one of these days.

As I step inside, I immediately notice Charlotte's absence. I groan. Of course, she did mention she was taking a prolonged weekend to visit some friends in Belfast. Instead of her usual happy, round face behind the counter, is that of Cassandra who normally only comes for later shifts. Cassandra is a little older than us, and although she's been in the industry for much longer, she doesn't seem to be able to keep up pace with the flow of our morning regulars. Judging by the overwhelmed look on her face right this second, she's about two chai lattes away from quitting on the spot.

I quickly step in behind the counter, offering her an encouraging, *we-got-this* smile, and turn to face the first of a rapidly growing line of customers. The morning rush hits me like a tidal wave of caffeine addicts, each with their unique order and slightly desperate eyes. I'm juggling coffee beans, milk jugs, and the constant ringing of the cash register. It's like a chaotic ballet, and I am not used to being the lead dancer in the room.

Amidst the flurry of orders in a brutally hectic start of the day, I catch a familiar face out of the corner of my eye. A familiar, annoying face.

Raf is an athletic and pretty attractive man, but he's so painfully aware of it that he's rather obnoxious and exhausting to be around. Unfortunately, he works at a restaurant just a few numbers down the street, so he comes here often.

He saunters up to the counter, his usual smirk playing on his lips. "Ellie, long time no see. How's life treating you?"

Okay, so we had a one-night stand. And I would love to just forget about it and pretend it never happened. Can we do that? I force a polite smile, desperately trying to push the cringeworthy memories to the back of my mind. "Hi Raf. Sorry, busy morning. What can I get you?"

Raf leans in, grinning smugly. "Surprise me, Ellie. I know you're full of surprises."

For the love of—.

It was a long time ago. Debbie and I went out for dinner once shortly after things ended with Elliott, and we stumbled upon that Italian place that Raf works at. And I am not *quite* sure what happened, but when I tried to make space for the plates he was about to place in front of us, shuffling our glasses and the romantic candle around, I spilled my wine all over myself and the tablecloth caught fire. Debbie grabbed the water carafe and splashed it on the flames first, then on my dress, and the worst was avoided (the "worst" being the fire spreading to the whole restaurant—on a personal level, my dress was forever ruined, so it was still a pretty big loss). It was a brand-new dress as well. But I guess I must have made a strong impression on Raf, because when I was done patting myself dry, he gave me his phone number and asked me out on a "hot date" (his words).

So, there he was, all sexy and confident and Italian, and I needed a rebound so we went on a date and I ended up at his place. But then things didn't quite work out and we concluded the night with more awkwardness than I bargained for. Now every time I see him, memories flood my mind, and not the pleasant kind.

Anyway, I don't have time for surprises right now. I decide to play it safe with a cappuccino, and invite him to step aside to let Cassandra take the next order while I whip up his drink. I have always managed to keep my calm under pressure, and it is not the first time the café gets this busy, but I can't help but find the insistent look on Raf's face really annoying. Eager to see the back of him, I rush the last step of the preparation and hand him over a steaming cup of cappuccino with a... *pear-ish*-shaped, definitely NOT heart-shape foam art on top.

Oh well.

Raf not so much looks down at his cup as contemplates it, seemingly lost in thoughts, then up at me again with a face I don't like.

"Is that a new foam art you're practising before pride month? I must admit it's rather uncanny. It's a shame I don't swing that way—as you well know. Unless... you're trying to tell me something else?"

What is he talking about?

I peer at his drink and realise in horror that what was supposed to be a heart-shaped foam art, and looked roughly like a pear a minute ago, now appears positively phallic.

Oh God.

"Sorry," I say hastily, thinking quick to extirpate myself from this nightmare. Cassandra's stress is palpable and I really did *not* need this hold-up. "Can I have that back for a second?"

I snatch Raf's cup from his hands and grab the cocoa sprinkler to cover the foam in an abnormally large amount of cocoa before slamming a plastic lid down on and handing the cup back over the counter. I concentrate on my breathing, erratic from my stress and my frustration, and keep my hand as steady as I can. Raf doesn't seem to notice, and after a few, interminable seconds, he grabs his cup and motions away from the counter.

"Thanks, Ellie. Well, I won't hold you up, you guys seem to have your hands pretty full today. I'll see you around."

I scowl under my breath. God, he's *so cringe*. I don't even spare him another glance as he steps out and I turn back to our line of customers, trying to ignore Cassandra's visible panic. But as the morning progresses and the flow of patrons finally falls down, the chaos in my brain continues to spill into my work.

The truth is, I was up late last night browsing job boards and editing my CV, and then I struggled to fall asleep. As much as I tried, I couldn't push away the worried thoughts about all my unsuccessful applications, or the upcoming rent and bills that would make another dent into my already rather thin savings.

My mind blank and out of focus, I barely take notice of Hugo approaching the counter. As he places his order, my mind registers the word "Americano" but then takes a detour somewhere along the way. My hands move on autopilot, grabbing a milk jug instead of hot water, and I pour a velvety stream of milk into the dark liquid.

"Um, excuse me? Ellie? I asked for an Americano, but I think this is becoming a flat white…"

I peer up at his voice and I can see polite confusion etched across his face. I look down at the frothy beverage that I'm still holding in my hands, and my eyes widen as I realise my mistake.

"Oh God, Hugo, sorry! Of course you did. My apologies—an Americano on the house coming right up!"

He chuckles, taking the mishap in stride. "Well, it's no big deal, but I've never been one to turn down a free drink!"

I give him a grateful smile, my cheeks flushing a bit, although I notice that my stress levels seem to drop ever so slightly as his presence brings a welcome distraction to my chaotic day. I glance at him from the corner of my eyes whilst I hastily prepare his usual coffee.

He's got dark, tousled hair, a chiselled jaw line and a smile that could charm the caffeine out of a coffee bean. He is tall, his broad shoulders impeccably drawn by a well-tailored navy-blue suit jacket, and although I can't see his shoes from here, I am sure they're brown and shiny and perfectly well kept. His voice matches his appearance, with a standard London accent, but with his olive skin and somewhat Mediterranean name, I suspect he must have French origins. Now that I take a closer look at him, he's like the human embodiment of the ideal cup of coffee—strong, comforting, and capable of making my heart race.

"Here you go. One freshly brewed Americano," I say, sliding the cup across the counter with an apologetic smile. "Sorry for the wait."

"Oh don't worry about it, there's no rush." He takes a sip, savouring the flavour. "Ah, perfection. Thank you, Ellie."

I let out a small laugh—okay, more like a giggle—, relieved that he's taking it so well. And indeed, he doesn't seem to be in a rush to leave today, which I'm not mad about. "Well, cheers to happy accidents, right?" I add, raising my hand in the air as if to make a toast—regretting it immediately, blood instantly flushing my cheeks at the ridicule of my remark.

What am I *doing*?

But Hugo smiles widely and raises his cup too. "To happy accidents."

My spirits much higher than they were a few minutes ago, I reluctantly turn away from him to greet the customers who have just walked in. Hugo leans against the counter, sipping his drink, and I can feel his gaze fixed on me. There's warmth in his eyes, like a hint of anticipation mixed with genuine interest. When I hand over the three cappuccinos to go and the line clears out again, Hugo comes back to face me in front of the till.

"You know, Ellie, I've been meaning to ask you something. I've been coming here for a while but we never really got to speak properly. Would you like to go out with me? Maybe Saturday night, if you're free?"

Well. I was not expecting this. I blink twice, unsure if I heard him correctly or if my confused, chaotic mind is playing tricks on me, which quite frankly seems rather likely seeing how little I've slept and how much coffee I've had today to compensate. Yet here he stands, silently, patiently, with extreme confidence and an encouraging smile.

Yes, I desperately want to say. But no, I can't.

"I would love to, Hugo," I reply, trying to make it very clear in my tone just how sorry I am. "But I already have plans that day. I play volleyball with some friends and we usually finish up pretty late. I could do Sunday?"

Hugo's smile widens. "Sunday it is, then. I can't wait. Do you like French tapas?"

"Can't say I have ever had French tapas, but I like the sound of it!"

"Perfect then. Let's meet outside the café at 8:00?"

I nod in agreement, and with a satisfied expression, Hugo finishes his coffee and takes off. It's not until he's disappeared out the door that I realise he didn't even ask for my number... He's just confident like that, I guess. Or old school. Either way, it's pretty sexy.

I turn my attention to the next customer, trying to contain my excitement and regain my composure—I don't think we can afford many more mistakes at the café today. But as resume my work, I can't help but feel my heart dance with anticipation.

I can't believe I got myself into a date with Americano Hugo.

And I can't believe Charlotte wasn't there to see it—although it's probably for the best. God knows she wouldn't have been able to stop herself from making some kind of knowing, embarrassing comments. I'll call her tonight, though. I can't keep this to myself.

A smile creeps up to my lips as I imagine the conversation (there *will* be some high-pitched shrieking in Irish tones), but it fades quickly as I sense some agitation a few feet next to me and I haste over to rescue an incredulous Cassandra from three young girls who seem to be enquiring about our bubble tea options.

FOUR

As I sit in front of my computer, editing the latest episode of Ellie's Track, I hear the familiar ping of a new email notification. I can't help but feel a pang of disappointment as I open up the latest job rejection that has just landed in my inbox. Ugh, seriously? Even at the weekend?!

I think about the recruiter on the other end of the email, who is evidently having a wonderful Sunday skimming through dozens of applications and rejecting the vast majority of them just like that, with one click. I know it's not personal, but still. It's like a never-ending parade of polite rejections and it's starting to take a toll on my confidence. But I refuse to let it crush my spirits. This is just a temporary setback, right? Something better is bound to come my way.

I take a deep breath, close the window and shift my focus back to the podcast.

The episode I'm editing features Guadalupe, a Cuban salsa dancer who gives classes on Southbank on weekends. She has this amazing accent and a contagious energy, bringing the heat and solar radiance of her native island all the way to grey and rainy London. Guadalupe only arrived in the UK a few months ago when the borders reopened after the pandemic. Moving here was her lifelong dream, and even though the transition has been tough, her voice oozes with determination and a passion for embracing this new chapter of her life. We chatted about London's nightlife, dating, and her dreams for the future.

"I want a family," she confessed, her voice tinged with uncertainty. "But who knows when and how that's going to happen? But a few years ago, my cousin and I took a trip to Spain and we froze our eggs there. I wanted to have options, you know? To be in control of my life and how I choose to live it. I don't know if there's a man out there for me, but it's good to know I don't need one until I'm ready."

Her words took me by surprise, maybe because she looks so young still—she's barely older than me, come to think of it. But she's right; life is unpredictable for all of us, after all.

My thoughts drift to Hugo and our date tonight. He hasn't been back at the café since he asked me out, and I can't help but wonder if our date is still on. Glancing at the time, I see it's only 3:00 p.m. The anticipation is real, and I find myself yearning for the evening to arrive.

I return my attention to the screen, resuming the edits on the podcast episode. We recorded it on Tuesday night, and I had hoped to get it to Guadalupe today. However, the noisy children playing in the nearby playground and the less-than-ideal lighting threw some hurdles my way. I also realised a bit too late that Guadalupe's long, wavy dark hair kept brushing against the microphone, which means the sound track needs a fair bit of work.

After two more hours of intense focus, I close my laptop and lean back in my chair. A headache is starting to creep up on me, and my back is aching. I make a mental note to finish the editing tomorrow, and I head to the bathroom to grab a paracetamol.

The bathroom, like the kitchen, is both small and basic. It's not the selling point of the flat, but it's got all I need. I even have a small bathtub, and whenever I have a morning to myself, I like to soak in a bath of rose-scented foam with a good book or a podcast and enjoy some me time.

I catch a glimpse of my tired face in the mirror. Oh my god, I look positively exhausted. Well, staring at a screen for four hours straight does take a toll. I splash some fresh water on my face, gently pat it dry, and take a second look.

Now, I've been working on practising self-love and positive affirmations to keep my mental health in check. So, I swiftly push away the critical thoughts that tend to pop up — those annoying ones about the pimples on my jaws and the size of my lips—and instead, open my mind to more flattering thoughts.

My wavy shoulder-length hair falls just right, framing my face in a way that I quite like. I have hazel eyes and long natural lashes that I always get complimented on back home. My friends often complain about the fortune they spend on getting their eyelashes and nails done. Well, luckily, I don't have to worry about that too much. Although, I do enjoy treating myself to a gel manicure every now and then, just to avoid the hassle of chipped nail polish during my shifts at the café.

As for my complexion, it's fair and somewhat pale, with slightly rosy cheeks that easily blush with emotion or when the temperature rises. My lips are very thin while my nose is a bit bigger than I'd prefer, with a slightly upturned shape that makes it undeniably the most prominent feature on my face. But hey, it's all part of what makes me unique, right? Besides, Hugo asked me out while I was right in the midst of a hectic shift, probably had a blank expression on my face and with my hair most likely all over the place. And of all days, that's when he asked me out! So, that's definitely a good sign.

And who knows, maybe we'll discover we have more in common than just a love for French food. Even if things turn out to be a bit awkward, I know Charlotte will have my back and keep Hugo's americanos flowing until the end of time while I hide in the kitchen or crouch below the counter.

Hopefully, it won't come to that.

How is that for a pep talk? Enough overthinking, Ellie. Just relax and go with the flow.

I take a few deep breaths, in and out, to get my anxiety under control. When I feel calmer, I start applying a light foundation, a touch of mascara, and choose a nude lipstick that I tuck away in my bag to apply at the last minute. Then, I make my way to my closet, contemplating what to wear.

My bedroom, tucked away from the main living space, falls more into the functional room category. It is north facing so it doesn't get as much light as the rest of the flat, and the bed, the closet and the extra rack of clothes make the face feel quite cluttered.

It's been a while since I've been on a date—months, actually. I'm not quite sure what the appropriate attire is for a cool spring night out. Plus, I have no clue what Hugo will be wearing—I've only ever seen him in his work clothes!

Let me think... I want something cute and put together, something stylish but not over the top. Although, if we're going to a French place, maybe I should make an extra effort? Hmm, I'm not sure my Mancunian charm can compete with the dazzling Parisian look, but hopefully I can find something that I feel comfortable in and that matches the vibe.

After some contemplation, I settle on a flowy floral dress that I absolutely *adore* but rarely have the chance to wear. I try on a denim jacket and slip into a pair of white sneakers, taking a step back to assess the final look. Yes, I think that will do just fine. At the very least, it's comfortable, and I feel pretty in it.

As I step out of my apartment about an hour later, a mix of nerves and excitement rushes through me. The evening air is crisp and refreshing, and as I make my way to the café, I feel a wave of relief when I spot Hugo already waiting, his hands in his pockets, with his back turned to me. As if he heard my footsteps in the quiet paved street, he turns around and a smile instantly lights up his face as he sees me approaching.

"Ellie, you look stunning," he says, his voice warm and genuine. I thank him with a smile and return the compliment. He looks very handsome indeed in his light-blue linen shirt and dark blue trousers.

"I booked a table at Boro Bistro," he adds as we start walking, him leading the way while keeping pace with me.

I've never been there myself, but I've heard it's excellent. Juliette mentioned it to Charlotte and me once and suggested we give it a try. When we arrive at the restaurant, the alluring aroma of delicious food welcomes us at the entrance. Since the evening is still warm, we settle into the cosy outdoor sofas near the heaters, and a friendly waiter presents us with the menu.

Hugo barely glances at the menu before looking up with a playful smile. "So, Ellie, are you an adventurous eater or more inclined to stick with your tried-and-true favourites?"

"I think I'm somewhere in between," I reply carefully. "I enjoy trying new things, but I also have a few go-to dishes that never disappoint. And you?"

"Well, my mum is French, so I wouldn't say this is adventurous because I got to sample this kind of food from quite a young age when we'd spend the summer at my gran's in Corsica."

I silently congratulate myself for my incredible deduction skills. There you go. French origins—I called it. Although it is doing nothing to calm down the butterflies that have taken residence in my stomach... and other places, too.

"But yes, I'm definitely an adventurous eater," he continues, unaware of the turmoil he's causing in me. "I love exploring different cuisines and flavours. Life's too short not to taste everything, right?"

I have a feeling that Hugo knows the entire menu like the back of his hand anyway, so it's no wonder he sounds so confident. It's uncharted territory for me, but I'm more than happy following his lead. And clearly, he has great taste—after all, he chose the best café in town for his morning coffee. Ha!

"You're absolutely right," I say with a smile, regaining my composure. "So, what would you recommend?"

"You have to try the duck potted meat," Hugo suggests. "And don't forget about their cheese selection. Do you like cheese?" He raises an eyebrow inquisitively.

"I love cheese," I assure him. "My goodness, everything looks so enticing. So *delicieux*. I wouldn't even know where to begin!"

He chuckles, his eyes sparkling. A waiter with a strong French accent approaches our table, and Hugo proceeds to order not just a few, but a generous variety of dishes along with a bottle of red wine. The waiter soon returns with two glasses of water and a basket of complimentary bread and butter for our table.

"Off to a great start," I nod approvingly.

I tear off a piece of bread, feeling Hugo's gaze on me as I intentionally avoid his eyes. It may be silly, but I can't help feeling oddly shy sitting across from this man in such a pleasant—dare I say, *romantic*—setting. The string lights and the clinking of wine glasses create an ambiance that's a far cry from the beige tiles and café chatter I am used to seeing Hugo in. Speaking of wine, a sip or two would certainly help calm my nerves.

Thankfully, the waiter returns with our bottle and two glasses, and Hugo raises his glass to me.

"Cheers," I say, finally meeting his eyes, as a warm sensation spreads through my stomach that has nothing to do with the wine.

Before I know it, a ballet of waiters descends upon our table, laying down an alarmingly large selection of the mouth-watering tapas that Hugo ordered for us to share.

"Are we expecting anyone else?" I jest, my eyes darting over the countless plates. I can't help but feel a twinge of remorse for the slices of delicious bread and butter I devoured while we were waiting.

"I don't think so," Hugo replies, visibly proud of himself. "I know it's a lot, but you *have* to try these. There was no other way! And didn't you mention playing a long game of volleyball in the heat?"

"Yes, I did. *Yesterday*," I reply. "That hardly counts as an excuse. But I don't think I will need much convincing to indulge in this fantastic display," I say as I scoop up a spoonful of *rillettes*.

We proceed to sample a variety of dishes, from succulent *croque-monsieur* oozing with cheese to a charcuterie board adorned with small pickled onions and cornichons. My excitement for all this French deliciousness may be a bit excessive, but Hugo seems to thoroughly enjoy watching me savour what seems like every single item on the menu. He suggests I take a bite of this and a spoonful of that, and I'm more than happy to oblige. His wishes are my command.

"I can't believe how amazing this is," I exclaim, relishing a bite of the creamy hummus. "It's like a flavour explosion in my mouth. You certainly know your way around good food, Hugo."

"Well, I have to admit, I'm a bit of a foodie," he confesses. "I love exploring new cuisines and trying unique dishes. French food is a particular favourite of mine, so when I discovered this place, it was a game changer. I've been coming practically every month since."

"So, what you're saying is that you're a man of habits?" I tease, raising an eyebrow. "Same café every day, same restaurant every month?"

"Are you calling me boring?" He laughs and tops up my wine glass. "So, tell me more about your podcast. What is it called again?" he asks with genuine interest.

"It's called Ellie's Track. I've been producing it for two years now."

"Wow, that's something."

"I really enjoy it," I admit, somewhat shyly, my cheeks feeling warm. "I didn't think too much about it when I first started, I just kept it going one episode at a time and here we are now. I'm even gaining a few followers every week," I add, feeling a lot more confident now.

"That is so cool!" Hugo exclaims, visibly impressed. "And where do you find your guests?"

"Everywhere! A lot of them I had met personally before, at the café or out and about in London. But listeners also suggest someone that they reckon has a good story to tell, and sometimes they're actually a very good match. I've even had a drag queen from Australia on the show once, they were touring the world with a show and I was invited backstage to record the podcast with them afterwards. That was one of the best episodes, actually."

"Wow, that sounds so good! Did you ever consider monetising it? If you have such an engaged community, I'm sure you could make some cash out of it," Hugo suggests.

"I'm not going to lie, I thought about it, especially after I lost my job," I admit. "But I don't think I want it to change in that way. I hate it when I'm listening to a podcast and the host is always advertising something, and I don't really want to ask my followers for money. It all started as a hobby for me, a way to connect with the world during the pandemic… it would feel wrong to make a profit from it, you know?"

He nods in understanding. "Well, who knows. Maybe you could still get a job out of it. It sounds like you're meeting great people and making connections."

The rest of the evening becomes a delightful blur of laughter, amusing anecdotes, and delectable dishes. When the desserts finally arrive and I catch sight of the decadent French chocolate mousse, I silently congratulate myself for choosing that flowy dress. Finally, after a solid team effort, all the plates, bowls and cups before us are empty and Hugo asks for our bill.

"I'll walk you home," he says as we exit Boro Bistro and he extends his hand in front of him, gently showing me the way. "*Après vous.*"

We continue our discussion as we stroll back past London Bridge station and into Bermondsey Street. It is still early and pubs are still open and packed, with patrons spilling over onto the dimly lit street. Hugo walks next to me, matching my pace, until he slows down and comes to a halt in the middle of the street.

"I used to live here," he explains in response to my inquisitive look, nodding towards a gate to our right. "In this building. I shared a small flat with three mates from uni. We had a lot of parties and barbecues on our small balcony in the summer," he adds, his face lighting up at the memory. "And there's a great view from the rooftop, too. I'm sure they haven't changed the codes."

He heads for the gate and starts dabbing at the gate keypad, and a second later, I hear a successful buzz and he leans against the gate, pushing it open with a triumphant *told you!* look on his face.

"Hugo, what are you *doing*?"

"Come on! I'll show you something."

I look around, half expecting someone to come and arrest us for trespassing, but not a single person is paying us any attention. And even if they were, why would they have any reason to think we're not supposed to be here? It's not like we're breaking and entering. We're just… entering.

Excitement takes over from my nervousness and I follow Hugo through the gate, into a courtyard and to the entrance door of one of the four buildings surrounding us. An instant later, there is a new buzz and Hugo holds the door open for me.

"How long ago did you say you lived here?" I ask as I follow him up a flight of stairs.

"I moved out a couple years ago, but I lived here for four years and the codes never changed in the whole time we were here."

He says that like it's the most natural thing and London is the safest place in the world, but I don't comment on it as I'm already panting a bit from climbing so many steps. Finally, we reach the top floor and I follow him as he steps over the metal chain bordering the pathway. I join him on the gravelled square and as he comes to a halt, looking around, so do I.

From this vantage point, the view is nothing short of breathtaking. The energy of the city pulsates around us, the night air, cool and crisp, carrying with it fragments of distant laughter and the faint screech of the late-night trains running a few hundred yards away.

To our right, majestic and bright, the towering silhouette of the Shard pierces through the night sky, casting an ethereal glow against the obsidian canvas above. I gaze up at this architectural marvel, with its sharp edges and sleek lines, standing tall and proud, as if it was reaching towards the heavens. From the moment I lay eyes on it, I become transfixed by the glow of its glass-clad façade. It is like a beacon in the night, its illuminated apex serving as a guiding light for those navigating the city's labyrinthine streets at night after a few drinks.

I can feel Hugo's electrifying presence besides me. I am afraid that if I speak, I will break the spell of this magic moment, so we remain silent for a while, lost in this moment of quiet reverence, soaking in the grandeur of the cityscape before us.

"Not bad, uh?" he says finally, his soft voice bringing me back to earth in the nicest possible way. "I used to come here a lot before I moved. I forgot how much I liked it."

"So this is not your first-date secret weapon then?"

He laughs, turning to face me. "No, it's not, I've never brought anyone here." He pauses, tilting his head, his eyes still fixated on me. "But if it was, would it be working?"

"Maybe."

He grins even more and the sight of the glimmer in his eyes and the dimples at the corner of his lips gives me goosebumps. Hugo must notice it and mistake them for shivering, because he frowns and takes his jacket off. "Come on," he says, draping it over my shoulders, "let's get you home."

We descend from our lofty perch, back through the courtyard and into the now quiet street below until we're back outside White Cuppa House.

"This way," I say, taking the lead to guide us the rest of the way. "This is me," I say when we reach my doorstep. I take off his jacket, reluctantly parting with it, its comforting smell still lingering around my neck and in my hair. "Thank you for such a wonderful evening."

"It was my absolute pleasure."

"I didn't think it was possible to eat so much charcuterie in one sitting."

He laughs. "We did have a lot, didn't we? Well, I'm glad you liked it." He pauses, his eyes locked with mine. "I had an amazing time tonight. I'd love to see you again. *Not* just at the café," he clarifies, his gaze unwavering.

A surge of happiness fills my heart, and I can't help but smile. "I'd love that too."

He smiles, visibly pleased, and after a short pause, he leans in invitingly. I catch his hint and meet him halfway, our lips coming together in a gentle, lingering kiss. It's sweet and soft and exciting — a perfect ending to a perfect evening. My breath accelerates, blood flushing my cheeks, but he's already pulling away gently, and our lips break apart. Kiss-drunk and longing for more, I blink in confusion before realising he's waiting for me to open the door and get inside before departing. I quickly grab my keys and find the fob to open the gate. He gives me one more of his devastatingly beautiful smiles and my hand a last little squeeze before turning around and walking away.

As I step inside, my heart is still pounding in my chest, and a bright smile refuses to leave my lips. It's late, but I feel perfectly awake. It's almost midnight now, but I'm not sure where the time went — I just know that I've been content with Hugo's company, and I can't wait to see him again. To kiss him again.

I sink into the plushness of my sofa, a stupid, blissful smile still on my face. My phone pings in my bag, and ignoring the five unread messages from Charlotte impatiently pleading for an update, I beam even wider as I find, at the top of the screen, the first message from the number I saved earlier in the evening.

"See you soon, Ellie."

FIVE

"Sooooooo you like him," Charlotte concludes with a wide grin on her face. You like Mr Americano Hugo."

She insisted on a minute-by-minute recap of my date with Hugo, and alright, I'll admit I was quite excited too, and to be fair to her, her gasps and interjections throughout my monologue were *on point*. But now that I've told her the whole story, I'm suddenly feeling weirdly nervous. I drop a kitchen towel on the counter with a sigh, placing my hand on my forehead.

"Maybe? Yes. I'm not sure. I think I might, but it was just one date. And I've had great first dates before that led me right into dead ends, so… you know. We'll see."

Clearly, that wasn't the response Charlotte was hoping for. "Oh come on now, Ellie! Don't be such a Debbie Downer. It sounds like you had an amazing time, just enjoy it!" She drops her elbows on the counter and leans into me, locking her eyes with mine. "How was the kiss? Was it good?"

I smile. "Yes, I confess. The kiss was good. Really good, actually. It was tender and sweet, and…."

Charlotte squeals in delight, clapping her hands together. "I knew it! I wouldn't have believed it if you had told me that Americano Hugo wasn't a great kisser, anyway. I mean, it's practically written on his face. Honestly, Ellie, I don't know how you're not head over heels for him right now, this is MAJOR news!"

I pause for a moment, taking a sip of my latte, lost in thought. If I'm being completely honest with myself, I feel like I *am* a bit head over heels for Hugo after the incredible evening we spent together.

How could I not? It was perfect. He is smart, cultivated, but also fun and cheeky—not to mention incredibly handsome. And, you know, not that it matters or anything, but I he seems to be doing very well professionally, too. He works at a company in Canary Wharf. He didn't tell me the name, but from what I gathered, they are doing great. They have been expanding rapidly in the past two years when every other business out here is struggling, and I think Hugo has a seat at the table of big discussions. Basically, worlds apart from my current situation.

He looked a bit taken aback when I shared my story of being made redundant and how I ended up at the café. His expression shifted momentarily when I mentioned my relentless search for another job and my savings running low, and for a moment I feared it might have changed his perception of me. But he then said he thought it was very brave of me to jump headfirst into a completely different career path and hold on to my dreams.

"Your current situation is not a reflection of who you are," he said seriously. "Circumstances can change, but it's the drive that matter."

And I know he's right and my career, or the lack thereof, doesn't define my worth. But honestly, *what* do I have to bring to the table? So of course, part of me is dying to see him again and explore the potential of our connection. I want to dive right into it and forget about everything else. But I feel so… inadequate compared to someone like him. And it's not just that—I don't even know if I can date anyone, at this point. Not now, when I still don't have a stable job, my savings are dwindling, and I have a million other things demanding my attention. Including…

"So, when are you seeing him again?" Charlotte asks relentlessly, dragging me out of my thoughts.

"I'm not sure. I'm headed to Manchester after my shift," I reply. "Remember, I'm off until next Thursday?"

It's my grandma's 90th birthday on Friday, and I'll be spending some time with my family up north. I haven't seen them since Christmas.

"Oooooh yes, I remember now," Charlotte says. "Gosh, that's rubbish timing, Ellie. But that's okay, I mean, I'm sure you'll text, right?"

"Yes, I suppose…" I reply cautiously. I hope we will.

I leave the café shortly before the lunchtime rush and hurry home to pack my suitcase for the week ahead.

Aboard the train to Manchester, I let thoughts of Hugo and of my conversation with Charlotte fill my head, weighing the pros and cons and trying to establish how I really feel about the whole situation. As it turns out, Hugo is quite a good texter, and from the few messages we've exchanged, he seems genuinely interested in me. He's even listened to a couple of episodes of Ellie's Track and he sounded quite impressed.

Mam, dad, and even my not-so-little brother Liam are already waiting for me when the train reaches Manchester Piccadilly.

"Mam, I swear you look younger every time I see you!" I exclaim, marvelling at her vibrant smile.

"Ellie, it's so wonderful to have you home," she responds, beaming with pride. "It's been far too long."

I blush, feeling the warmth of their love. "I've missed you all too. How is Grandma? Is everything ready for the big day?"

"Almost," Dad chimes in, leading us towards the exit. "Your Nan is all settled in Liam's old room. Her sisters will arrive on the morning train tomorrow and will stay with Agnes and George, but otherwise, everything is ready and everyone is excited. The weather forecast looks promising, so we should be able to spend some time in the garden."

As we make our way to the car, my heart feels lighter, all thoughts about Hugo and my precarious work situation completely vanished. When we reach home, I'm pleasantly surprised to find a few more relatives who were holding the fort while my parents and Liam came to pick me up.

The dinner table is set in the winter garden, and Dad gestures for me to take a seat while he takes my suitcase upstairs. The delectable aroma of home-cooked food fills the air, making my stomach grumble with anticipation. Aunt Agnes, Dad's sister and a culinary genius, has prepared a welcoming feast for all of us. And as I glance at what's simmering on the stove, a grin spreads across my face.

"Aunt Agnes, do you remember when I was five, and you accidentally spilled spaghetti all over me? Will I get to eat them from a plate tonight?" I tease her.

Aunt Agnes bursts into laughter, her eyes crinkling with mirth. "Oh dear! Of course, I remember! That was quite the spectacle. I think your Mam still has a picture of you somewhere, covered in noodles from head to toe. What can I say? I'm a little clumsy!"

"And let's not forget the time Liam tried to feed the dog cauliflower cheese and gravy!" Uncle George joins in.

Liam's cheeks flush, turning a shade of crimson. "Hey! It seemed like a good idea at the time! Gary looked like he wanted a taste!"

"And here she is, the queen of the week!" Dad announces, his hand proudly supporting Grandma's arm.

"Nan!"

Grandma's face lights up when she sees me, and I embrace her in a warm, tight hug. Even at the youthful age of 90, she still has the elegance and warmth of a silver screen goddess. Time has gracefully etched its mark upon her face, but she embraces her age with pride, wearing her wisdom and resilience like badges of honour. Her emerald eyes still hold a mischievous twinkle, hinting at the secrets she may still have up her sleeve, and her silver mane, impeccably styled, tells tales of a lifetime filled with remarkable stories and experiences. Her hands, delicately weathered, have nurtured and cooked for her loved ones for countless years. Petite and plump, she exudes timeless elegance with a dash of contemporary flair.

Today, she's wearing chic pantsuits and a red-and-white polka-dotted silk scarf. Tucked away underneath, I know she wears a golden locket containing a black-and-white photograph of my grandfather. He passed away more than thirty years ago, but whenever his name comes up in conversation, her eyes glisten with an extra sparkle.

"It's so good to see you, Nan,"

"You've lost weight," she replies, pinching my cheeks. "Do you eat enough in London?"

"Yes, I eat plenty," I reply, choosing not to remark that comments on weight are not something we do any more—or shouldn't. "I spend a lot more time standing up than I used to, that's all."

"Well, we better all sit down and start eating before it gets cold," Aunt Agnes chimes in, carrying a tray of homemade garlic bread fresh out of the oven.

We gather around the dining table, passing plates filled with love and the unmistakeable savours of my favourite family recipes. Nan is sitting across me, glowing. She is the heart and soul of our clan, and I feel so lucky to get to celebrate her life and still have her by our sides. She raised my dad and his siblings with unwavering dedication to traditional family values, and in turn, my parents have passed down those values to Liam and me. While London has been my home for the past five years, and I cherish my friends and the life I've built there, the rollercoaster of setbacks and challenges has left me feeling somewhat lonely at times.

After dinner, exhausted from a long day and ready to slide into a blissful food coma, I drag myself up the stairs and collapse onto my bed. It's been over a decade since I've moved out, and my parents have since transformed what used to be my bedroom into a storage-slash-guest room. But the wooden furniture and wallpapers remain the same, and the air still carries the familiar scent of my old room.

I reach into the pocket of my coat and retrieve my phone, a smile sneaking onto my face as I open my new messages and spot one from Hugo.

"Did you make it home okay? How's Manchester treating you?"

I quickly type a reply: "I feel like my stomach is about to explode! Just had a big family dinner and it's only the beginning, but it's so nice to see everyone again after so long. My brother teased me the whole night on my accent, he says I sound posh like Gillian Anderson now."

I've barely had time to change into my pyjamas that the screen lights up again.

"Haha! That's the ultimate sign of a true Londoner. Enjoy the festivities, and I can't wait to hear all about it when you're back."

My smile widens as I plug my phone to charge and set my alarm for tomorrow morning. I'm looking forward to spending a few days up north with all my loved ones, but I do have to say, Charlotte was kind of right about the rubbish timing of it all. Because I *am* really excited to see him again. It scares me to admit it, even more so to myself, but the way I get all jumpy and giggly like a teenager when my screen lights up with his name is a sure tell-tale.

SIX

"We're going to need more matches."

Liam shakes his wrist and as the flame turns into a thin thread of smoke, he discards the little piece of burnt wood to the side of the table to join the two dozen used matches already lying there.

As Nan's only grandchildren, him and I are tasked with the monumental challenge of lighting up the candles. All ninety candles in play. Oh yes, we insisted on it—ninety lights to dazzle and shine. But here's the catch: however enormous this cake is, finding space for those last dozen candles is nothing short of a perilous game of culinary Jenga—with an added layer of a fire hazard.

But Nan's birthday cake is a showstopper like no other. Picture this: a custom-made three-tier creation, lovingly handpicked by Dad from our local bakery this very morning. It's a symphony of raspberries, strawberries, and heavenly vanilla cream, Nan's favourite. And on top of that sugary mount, there are these exquisite sugar pearls and roses, along with a sheet of almond paste and chocolate, spelling out the words "Happy Birthday Irene." Honestly, if I ever get married, I want an exact replica of this masterpiece.

The last couple of days have whirled by in a delightful tornado of family chaos. It's been a frenzy of tight hugs and infectious laughter, each day bringing its share of delicious Yorkshire pudding, gravy and other delicious fish pies Mam and Aunt Agnes whip up for us all. And now, the big day is upon us, and all of our closest relatives are chattering in the garden under the radiant sun, waiting for the dessert.

Finally, with the cake held precariously in our hands, we step out of the house and approach Nan, her face beaming with sheer joy and pride. Her eyes tear up, the ninety lights twinkling in them like dancing fireflies. And just as we draw closer, the entire family bursts into a rousing chorus of "Happy Birthday." The air reverberates with our heartfelt melody, and time seems to pause, basking in the overwhelming love we shower upon our Nan.

My heart swells with affection as I gaze at her, battling an emotional tsunami threatening to make me wobble and turn this towering cream confection into a colossal mess. I gather my resolve, steadying myself like a master tightrope walker, determined not to drop this edible masterpiece before it safely reaches the table.

Uncle George pops open a bottle of bubbly, and Aunt Agnes circulates around the gathered guests, offering steaming cups of coffee and tea. Dad, Liam, and I spring into a well-orchestrated routine, Dad slicing the cake with finesse, Liam expertly passing the plates, and me gliding them over to our relatives.

"Here you go, Nan," I announce, presenting her with a generously sized slice adorned with a mountain of cream. "Mind the cream, I wouldn't want it to stain your new scarf!"

"Oh, my darling Ellie, thank you ever so much. I've been truly spoiled, not just with these marvellous gifts but by having all of you here today. Even Margie and Ann left the retirement home for the occasion, I wasn't expecting them here."

Margie and Ann are Nan's oldest friends, and although Ann is now increasingly deaf and Margie struggles to stand without her walker, the sight of the three of them together always makes me tear up. No matter the amount of time that passes, these three are bonded with an indefectible friendship that I envy Nan for.

"Don't be silly, of course, we're all here! We wouldn't miss it for the world," I assure her, genuinely. "I am glad you're happy, and you liked your gifts."

Liam joins us, offering each of us a glass of sparkling wine. Nan lovingly caresses her new pear-shaped golden brooch, glinting brightly against her vibrant red cardigan. "I love them," she says, her voice filled with affection. She leans closer and adds, "But you know what the greatest gift would be? Make me a great-grandma before my time is up, will you?"

Liam bursts into laughter while I gasp. "Nan! Don't even think about such things. You're going to live forever," I say, categorically. "Besides, if anyone should be asked, it's Liam! He's been with his girlfriend for five years, hasn't he?"

Liam's laughter subsides immediately, and he raises his hands in surrender. "Easy there, Sis! All in good time," he replies, his eyes darting towards Orla, his long-term girlfriend, who feigns innocence while sipping her tea.

Now, why would she turn down the glass of prosecco Dad offered her alongside her slice of cake? That's not like her... Not that I would ever bring up the baby topic myself, though. Maternity is a very personal choice, and I have met with enough women with difficult journeys on my podcast to know better than to ask my own brother's girlfriend about it. No way.

Evidently, Liam has a different perspective on respecting his sister's personal matters' privacy.

"But yes, what about you, Ellie? Are you seeing anyone? Have you met someone special?" he asks as we settle back into our seats next to Mam and Dad, who suddenly perk up, not hiding their interest in the conversation.

I wave off his question with a dismissive gesture. "Ah, I don't know. It's not the best time for it, is it?"

"Depends," Liam says through a mouthful of cake. "If they're taking you out to dinner and offer a place to shower, I'd say it's a prime time for it."

"That's... modern," I reply as dad snorts. "But not a terrible idea, I suppose."

Mam frowns, looking concerned. "Are you struggling with money, Ellie? If you need some support, you know we're here for you."

"*No*, Mam, I'm grand, don't worry!" I reply quickly. "Well, not yet, anyway. I *may* have dipped into my savings a bit, but it's just temporary. Something will come up soon. Positive vibes and all that!"

I smile widely, feeling a twinge of guilt while trying to convince both Mam and myself that I have it all under control. I've always prided myself on my independence, always managed to find my way through rough patches. This is just another bump on the road, and I'm determined to navigate it with confidence and my head held high.

"Have you considered moving out?" Dad chimes in. "You could find a nice flat share…"

"Or you can move back home, if you want. We'd be more than happy to have you."

I blink in surprise at Mam's suggestion, unsure if I heard her correctly. The table falls silent, and Liam shoots me an uncertain look. A heavy feeling settles in the pit of my stomach.

"I'm not moving back here, Mam," I reply, my tone more defensive than intended. "My life is in London. I'm making some money, still have savings. I've got this. I'll figure it out."

"But what if it takes longer than expected? What if it's another six months?" Mam's voice is filled with concern. "I'm not saying it's your fault, love, or that you're not trying your best. It's just tough out there. If you moved back home, you could save money while still searching for jobs in Lon—"

"I'll… I'll think about it," I say, my words trailing off uncertainly. I grab a generous forkful of cake and stuff it into my mouth. Mam catches the hint and drops the subject, taking a sip of her coffee.

I know she means well, and truth be told, I've pondered the idea myself on my darkest days—those days of relentless rejections, usually amplified by a severe case of PMS. Coming back home would be the sensible thing to do, and if I don't find a higher-paying job very soon, I won't have another choice but to leave my current flat for a more affordable place. But deep down, I can't bear the thought. I really hope it doesn't come to it.

As the afternoon winds down, the guests depart and hug Nan goodbye, promising to visit again soon. Liam and Dad pack away the garden furniture, Mam starts boxing up the leftovers, and I diligently dry the dishes passed to me by Uncle George.

Lost in my own thoughts, I can't shake off Mam's concerned gaze and her words.

What if she's right? What if I really have to leave my life in London and all the promises I made myself behind?

SEVEN

The birthday celebrations have faded away, and peace and quiet settle down the house. I'm barely able to summon the energy—or find the room in my belly—to meet up with my old girlfriends for brunch on Sunday. It isn't until Monday night, when Mam, Dad, Nan, Liam, Orla, and I gather at the pub for a final dinner together, that I venture out again.

The next morning, Liam drops me off at the station on his way to work and I board the 8:55 train to London Euston. As I arrive, the sun beams down on me, as if to welcome me back with open arms. I make a firm resolution to spend the afternoon strolling along Southbank, relishing the chance to be a tourist in my own city.

Filled with energy at the thought of my leisurely walk, I swiftly drop off my suitcase at home, start a load of laundry, give my plants a good watering, and change into lighter attire. With an extra bounce in my stride, I step back outside, ready to conquer the day. Bermondsey Street is quieter on weekdays, and as I pass by White Cuppa House, I catch a glimpse of Cassandra looking incredibly bored behind the counter.

I pick up the pace, eager to reach Bankside and soak in the view of the Tower of London and St Paul's Cathedral across the river.

Further down, as I approach Shakespeare's Globe, I start recognising the familiar faces of the tour guides and street artists who frequent this area, entertaining new batches of tourists each day, their enthusiasm unbridled.

By the OXO Tower, just as I contemplate my choice between the classic combination of pistachio and chocolate sorbet and a more adventurous gelato flavour, my phone starts buzzing. A strange sensation tugs at my stomach as I see Hugo's name flashing on the screen, and I quickly step to the side to answer the call.

"Hello?"

"Hey, you! How's it going?" he greets me cheerfully. "Did you make it back okay?"

"Yeah, all good, thanks. I arrived around lunchtime and have been strolling around London this afternoon. And actually, your timing is perfect, because I'm currently debating ice cream flavours," I add playfully. "Any recommendations?"

"Hmm, how about something fresh and herby? Do they have a basil and lime option?"

"They do, actually," I reply, rather impressed. I knew he had good taste, but I didn't expect him to be a gelato connoisseur.

"Then I'd go for that and pair it with something like fig yoghurt. Let me know what you think. On another note, what are your plans for the rest of the day?"

"Nothing much," I reply, intrigued. "Why?"

"I was thinking we could sit in a park or grab drinks somewhere. It's too nice to be cooped up indoors any longer. Work can wait until tomorrow," he suggests enthusiastically.

"Uh… Okay, yes, sure!" I respond, feeling a delightful thrill. "I'd love that. Where should I meet you?"

"How about the Cutty Sark at 6:00 p.m.?"

I check the time on my phone—it's just past five. It's going to be tight, but I'll make it work. "Perfect, I'll see you then!"

I hang up the phone and stand there for a moment, processing the new whirlwind of emotions Hugo's phone call just stirred up inside me. *God, what is happening?* It's been a while since I felt these little butterflies fluttering in my stomach, and I don't *not* like it, but it's… a lot.

I take another quick glance at the Gelateria and realise my appetite has suddenly vanished, so I turn around, hastening my pace towards the tube station.

***

With five minutes to spare, I arrive at our meeting spot and notice Hugo already standing by the entrance of the Greenwich tunnel, gazing up at the towering boat that casts its majestic shadow on the pavement. He is wearing an elegant navy-blue suit with a linen white shirt, his jacket casually thrown over his shoulder, and I feel a bit underdressed in comparison in my stripy jumpsuit and flat sandals.

"There you are," Hugo says when he sees me. He doesn't hesitate when he gives me a quick kiss on the lips, and although I can feel a blush flushing my cheeks, I am relieved at how naturally it came to him.

"Shall we?" he says, showing me the way towards Greenwich Park.

The walk up the hill isn't easy in this heat and shoes, but the viewpoint is always worth it. From up here, it looks as if the city has spread itself out just to impress us, showing off its architectural prowess and historical treasures.

To the north, the Shard shoots up into the sky, catching the sunlight and sparkling like a giant disco ball, just as majestic in broad daylight as it is at night. Peeking behind it, St Paul's Cathedral stands tall and proud, like an elegant diva demanding attention.

My eyes dance across the horizon, tracing the winding path of the River Thames. Uber boats glide along the river, transporting high-end commuters from one side to the other. Tower Bridge takes centre stage, with those magnificent towers and suspended walkways. It's a shame it's still daylight—there is nothing quite like the sight of an illuminated Tower Bridge at night.

Further west is the grand entrance of the Houses of Parliament, with Big Ben chiming away every hour in the brand new, entirely renovated Elisabeth Tower. Down on Westminster Bridge, although we can't see them from up here, I can only imagine the symphony of red double-decker buses, black taxis, and eager tourists buzzing around like busy bees in a honey pot. Finally, turning east, our eyes meet the futuristic skyline of Canary Wharf, standing tall and proud. It's like a scene from a sci-fi movie, with those shiny glass skyscrapers reaching for the stars. It's London's way of saying, "Hey world, we mean business!"

All the urban hustle and bustle contrasts with the lush greenery of Greenwich Park itself, with its leafy trees and velvety lawns. And right next to us, perched on the hill like a wise old sage, is the Royal Observatory and its courtyard, the Greenwich Prime Meridian imprinted on the pavement, standing over the course of time.

I can't help myself and take out my phone to capture a short video of the view and upload it to my Instagram story. When I put my phone away again and turn to face Hugo, he's looking at me, amused.

"What?"

"Nothing."

"My parents like to see what I'm up to in London," I explain, trying to concede my slight embarrassment. "They always ask me about my life here."

"Weren't you still with them just this morning?" he chuckles.

"And Nan is always the first one to like what I post," I continue, ignoring his comment.

"Your *Nan* is on Instagram?" Hugo asks, his eyes widening with surprise.

"Of course! Everyone's on Instagram these days," I shrug.

"I'm not," he counters. "I mean, I used to be, but not any more. Too much time wasted."

Now it's my turn to be surprised, although I shouldn't be. It makes sense that someone like Hugo would stay clear from social media and just live in the moment. I don't think he has anything to prove to anyone.

He probably reads a lot of inspirational books and wakes up at 5:00 a.m. to start the day off with his miracle morning routine or something.

We sit down on a bench and stay there for a while, admiring the view and talking about what we like, what we love, my trip to Manchester, and his plans for the summer (a two-week road trip through Ireland with a few friends and a week in Corsica). We talk about anything and everything, except for his work. Every time the subject has come up and I've asked questions about what he does, he's been pretty elusive. Maybe he prefers not bringing the stress and worries from work into his private life—I can understand that.

The sun is setting and as Hugo sees me shiver a little, he places his jacket on my shoulders like he did last time.

"Are you getting hungry?" he asks. "Or are you still full from your gelato?"

"I could eat," I confess, suddenly becoming aware of my grumbling stomach. I didn't tell Hugo that I never had that gelato in the end, and the small sandwich and few strawberries I had at lunch feel like an old memory after all that walking today.

"There is a pub nearby that we could go to if you'd like. It's not too far—my mates and I found it one day after a run in the park. Their food is fantastic."

I don't even need to try the food to know that The Plume of Feathers was a great choice—and also, I am pretty starved at this point, so I'm not going to be picky. The smell of food assailing us from everywhere as soon as we leave the park is practically torture, but thankfully, the pub we are headed to isn't far.

I feel an instant warmth embrace me the moment Hugo opens the door for me. Located on a quaint cobblestone street, The Plume of the Feathers is a charming blend of traditional and contemporary, like a modern-day Jane Austen novel brought to life. If they could talk, there is no doubt that the walls, adorned with vintage paintings and rustic wooden panels, would whisper scandalous tales of bygone eras.

The ambiance is lively yet cosy, with the soft glow of dimmed chandeliers casting a romantic aura over the room. The bar, polished to a high gleam, showcases an impressive array of spirits that would make any connoisseur swoon. From the amber hues of aged whiskies to the vibrant shades of craft gins, the bar holds the promise of liquid alchemy. Yet as is often the case, the colourful bottles remain almost untouched, some of them visibly covered in a small layer of dust, as regulars and tourists alike prefer the comfort and volume of a large draught pint of lager or IPA.

Waiters expertly balance plates of delicious food across the room and to the winter garden, and by the time the maître d' shows us to our seats, my mouth is salivating profusely.

"They certainly know how to market themselves," I remark, scanning the menu with amusement. "Listen to this: '*At The Plume of Feathers, we pride ourselves on our culinary offerings, marrying all your favourite traditional pub classics with our innovative twists. From sizzling fish and chips to sumptuous Sunday roasts, each of our dishes is a symphony of flavours that will leave your taste buds tingling with delight.*' Quite the statement."

"They're not exaggerating, I assure you," Hugo responds confidently.

We order food and pick up our conversation where we left it, effortlessly flowing from one topic to another. The lively ambiance of the pub requires us to raise our voices, and with each word he speaks, I find myself growing increasingly fond of his subtle southern French accent. I hadn't noticed it at first, but have become aware of it since he's mentioned his origins, and the way he says my name dives me goosebumps every time.

After a delicious dinner—chicken and mushroom pie for me, fish and chips for Hugo, and a heavenly sticky toffee pudding to share—, Hugo picks up the bill again and we start heading back.

"I'll walk you home," he announces again as we get off at London Bridge station.

"Are you sure? You don't have to—"

"Of course I'm sure! It's not far from mine anyway."

"And here I thought you were taking a long detour on your morning commute just to get a cup of the best coffee in town," I sigh playfully.

"When I moved out from the flat in the building I showed you last time, I only moved a few streets down. Sorry to burst your bubble," he adds, catching the look on my face. "I hope you're not too disappointed."

"I am, actually. Devastated."

We walk on autopilot through our neighbourhood until we reach the entrance of my building. I return his jacket to him and he throws it distractedly over his shoulder with a faint "thanks", his gaze fixated on me. The glow of a nearby streetlight reflects in his eyes, gleaming like the moon and intensifying the familiar burn that courses through me. "Do you…" I hesitate, my voice betraying me. Thank God it is dark, because my cheeks must be a vivid shade of crimson. Forget cute rosy cheeks; I'm giving you a full-on Pantone 200. I take a deep breath. "Would you like to come in?"

Hugo responds with one of his disarmingly charming smiles, followed by an eloquent kiss.

"Yes, I'd love that."

The jingle of my keys barely covers the cacophony of my heart pounding in my chest as I unlock the door to let us in.

EIGHT

Well, my clothes are definitely in need of rewashing if I don't want to stink like a wet dog the next time I wear them. Thankfully, at least my underwear isn't hanging up on display for Hugo to see as he walks into the room.

"Um... I'm sorry about the mess," I apologise as I start fumbling around the room, quickly taking in my open suitcase on the floor and the haphazardly thrown clothes scattered over the sofa. "I didn't expect to come home so late. Or to have company," I add, flustered.

Embarrassment sets my cheeks ablaze as I quickly switch on the lamp. I really didn't think this through, and I become painfully aware of my breath, my tongue feeling dry from the red wine and all the sugar and salt. Instinctively, I reach for the matches to light the candle, but then I pause, realising how that might come across. Instead, I grab the cardigan I left on the arm of the sofa earlier, hastily gather the rest of my clothes into a bundle, and hurriedly stuff them back into my suitcase, slamming the lid shut. Well, that's a bit better, I suppose.

"Would you like something to drink?" I offer, attempting to redirect the focus. "Water, wine, tea?"

Hugo doesn't respond with words, but he takes a step towards me, and as he gets closer, a warm shiver runs through my body. His perfectly sculpted hands reach out, lightly brushing my lips with his fingertips, cupping my face as he leans in. Time seems to freeze, the universe holding its breath in anticipation.

So do I.

And then, his lips, so soft and warm, meet mine in a tender kiss, sending an electric shock through my veins. His palms leave my face, travelling down to rest in the middle of my back, and our bodies naturally gravitate towards each other, deepening the connection of our kiss. After a moment, his hands move up my arms in a gentle caress, his fingers grazing my neck. Taking his subtle hint, I swiftly discard the cardigan I just put on a minute ago, flinging it to the corner of the room, leaving no doubt about my views on the so-called third-date rule. I feel his smile against my lips as he undoes the top buttons of his shirt, and we briefly break apart, giving me the chance to take in the sight before me.

My gaze travels down from Hugo's intense blue eyes to his now-bare chest, rising and falling rhythmically with each ragged breath. Every inch of his physique tells a story of strength and vitality, exuding timeless masculinity like a Greek sculpture brought to life. His skin, sun-kissed, boasts a bronzed hue, while his taut muscles ripple beneath the surface. Trailing from the centre of his chest, a smattering of dark, velvety hair creates an irresistible contrast against the hardness of his physique, a captivating juxtaposition that entices all my senses. It's as if his body holds the promise of both tender caresses and passionate embraces.

I find myself drawn to the gentle curve of his collarbones, delicate bridges connecting two worlds, leading me towards his neck, where the pulse of life beats steadily, luring me to explore further. His scent drugging me, my fingers tracing the lines and dips of his bare chest, desire surges within me. I peel off my jumpsuit, the warmth of his skin against my touch igniting a fire within me, a desire that burns with an intensity matched only by the blaze in his eyes.

Hugo's strong hands seize my thighs, lifting and wrapping them around his waist as he guides us towards the sofa. Our breaths synchronise, and gradually, lost in our embrace, the barriers between us dissolve, giving way to a raw vulnerability that takes hold. My hand instinctively ventures down his trousers, drawn to his visible desire, and his gasp sends a surge of exhilaration through my veins. My mind briefly flits to the bed side table in the other room, contemplating the logistics of the move, but before I can decide, Hugo retrieves what we need from his wallet.

In a swift moment, a small piece of foil and the rest of clothes join the scattered mess on the floor, and Hugo's powerful form looms over me. As natural as if we had already come together a million times before, I surrender myself to him completely.

***

A piercing sound jolts me awake from the hazy, blissful slumber I slipped into what feels like mere minutes ago.

"Wh—What is this?!"

Panicked, I scan the room, desperate to locate the source of this horrendous noise and silence it immediately.

Sometime during the night, we migrated to my bedroom, indulging in further exploration of our bodies until exhaustion lulled us to sleep. My hair is a mess, my skin still feels sticky from our combined sweat, but if popular belief holds true, I must be radiating a post-passionate glow. Just moments ago, I was tangled in Hugo's embrace, and whoever is responsible for this abrupt awakening deserves nothing short of a miserable day.

As it turns out, it is just Hugo's phone alarm. Hugo stirs beside me, finds his phone on the floor and instantly the glaring sound stops.

Thank God.

"I think I prefer the sound of crashing waves or birds in the forest," I croak, my voice still heavy with sleep.

"I know it's awful. Sorry," he apologises, "That's just an extra safety measure to make sure I don't sleep through it."

"What time is it?"

"It's 6:30. I should get going."

"But it's so early!" I protest, the remnants of sleep clouding my thoughts.

Hugo looks at me with a fond smile and leans a soft kiss on my cheek. "It bloody is, but I need to go home and get ready for work."

I pout in disappointment. He is definitely not a snoozer, this one. In an instant, he's up, running his fingers through his tousled hair and rubbing his face with fatigue evident in his movements.

"Well, that's terribly unfortunate," I reply, dramatically rolling over in bed, playfully tugging the sheet down my stomach. Hugo freezes, his eyes fixated on my exposed skin, but he releases a deep, resigned sigh and averts his gaze, heading towards the living room to gather his clothes. He returns a moment later, already fully dressed, and sits next to me on the bed.

"I'll see you soon?" he asks, his hand caressing my cheek, tucking a stray strand of hair behind my ear.

"Yes," I respond immediately, sighing contentedly, relishing the warmth of his touch.

I feel the weight of his body lift from the bed as he stands, his footsteps carrying him out of the room. Reluctantly, I throw on my robe and follow him to the living room to see him out.

Jesus. The room appears even messier now, my jumpsuit, cardigan and underwear discarded on the floor and the sofa pillows knocking about haphazardly. Hugo doesn't seem to mind though—I mean, he *did* contribute to some of the mess. In the most positive way possible.

"I had a great time last night, in case it wasn't glaringly obvious," he says as I join him by the door.

"Me too. Go on then, you're going to be late," I add, trying to play it cool even though I am pretty sure I am not fooling anyone.

"Is my favourite barista working today?"

I can't help but smile at the fond nickname. "Nope, I happen to know she's taking a well-deserved rest and returning straight to bed. But I'm sure Charlotte will take care of you, Mr Americano."

"Is that what you've christened me?" his eyebrows rising in surprise.

"Yep. You're Americano Hugo."

He throws his head backwards with a laugh that makes my heart melt. "I've been called far worse things, and I quite like this one." He plants a kiss on my lips and opens the door. "Enjoy your lie in for me."

And just like that, he's gone.

I close the door behind him, listening to his fading footsteps as they descend the stairs, before finally returning to bed. The sun shines brightly through the windows, but exhaustion overtakes me, and I drift back to sleep almost instantly.

When I wake up again a couple hours later, I linger in bed for a moment, processing.

Did I dream all this, or was Hugo really here, lying next to me? Embracing me? I reach out for the vacant pillow, and like a drug addict, I bury my face in it. Hugo's scent is imprinted on the fabric, and I can't stop inhaling it deeply, each whiff bringing back the memories of last night and his body pressed against mine.

He's probably already well on his way to work right this second. I wonder if he managed to grab his morning drink or if he was running too late for it. My mind drifts to the café and to Charlotte, who must be preparing Mrs Tucker's extra loaded skinny cappuccino. The usual bustle of Bermondsey Street is reaching my ears—a reminder that the world around me is wide awake and well on its way to another busy day.

And here I am, still nestled in bed, a thousand thoughts buzzing in my head like a swarm of bees. Thoughts clash within me, colliding, warring against one another. Mam's words echo inside my head; Hugo's face dances in my mind. I almost want to reach for his face and run my fingers through his tousled hair. His sea-blue eyes are staring into mine—he feels so close, and yet so far.

I grow all nervous and fidgety and jump out of bed, trying to brace myself for another day of relentless applications. But as I turn on my laptop, I make the foolish mistake of taking a quick glance at my bank account. My heart sinks as I lay eyes on my balance. How can my savings have dwindled away so quickly?

As if on cue, a new rejection email drops into my mailbox. Anxiety ripples through my body and I shiver. I'm stunned and slightly out of breath, as if I had just come out of a cold shower. The blissful feeling of waking up next to Hugo is long gone now, and I can't help but feel guilty for allowing myself to get sidetracked by this… fling.

Or whatever this is.

I don't know how long this thing with Hugo is going to last, but there is one thing I do know for sure: If I don't sort out my job situation soon, I'll have to end my long-term relationship with my flat, and that's the kind of heartbreak I am not ready for.

NINE

Okay, let's do this.

An hour later, I'm sitting in my sofa, fresh out of the bath and equipped with the emotional support of a large cup of coffee, ready to tackle the mind-numbing task of sorting through my pending applications and facing the cruel rejections that await me. Before I dive into the abyss of job hunting, I set a 30-minute timer. It's a nifty trick I picked up somewhere, and let me tell you, it works like a charm. Breaking up these never-ending tasks into bite-sized sprints keeps me focused and stops my mind from wandering off too far.

I start diligently logging updates on each job application, determined not to let the mounting rejections dampen my spirit. I conjure up my inner J. K. Rowling, reminding myself that even she faced many brutal rejections before someone finally recognised her wizardry and plucked her out of the slush pile.

I'm a bit of a dreamer when it comes to my career, too, holding on to the hope that somewhere out there, a job is waiting for me, just as eager to find its perfect match, and that one day not too far from now, we'll collide.

When the timer beeps, it's like a sudden jolt back to reality and it takes me a second to regain my bearings. I'm in the midst of crafting a cover letter for a junior after-effects designer role, and I might as well finish it before taking a well-deserved break.

My email sent, I shuffle to the kitchen to top up my cup of instant coffee—*no one* at White Cuppa House can *ever* find out about this. It's my dirty little secret.

Armed with my caffeine fix, I return to the living room, where the sun is practically begging me to come outside and frolic in its golden rays. But alas, duty calls, and a nagging voice in my head guilt-trips me into staying put and embarking into another few 30-minute sprints today.

I sink into the comforting embrace of the sofa, releasing a deep sigh, and mechanically refresh the LinkedIn page on my screen. The algorithm brings up a two-day-old post from Debbie who apparently attended some sort of conference in Dublin and is now *"so grateful to have had the opportunity to meet industry experts and learn from the best"*.

I can't help but snort at the sheer insincerity dripping from her words. I can accurately picture her face as she typed that post. Debbie and I once suffered through an online presence and personal branding course at Banders, and let me tell you, her expression screamed: *"I really can't be bothered with any of this, but if it can get me out of here, fine, I'll do it."* She's never been Banders' biggest fan, but as a member of the PR team, she has to put on a show and be the queen of fake enthusiasm.

I miss Debbie! We've been meaning to catch up for ages now… I grab my phone and swiftly type a message. "Hey, girl! It feels like forever! How've you been? Fancy meeting up for a gossip session over dinner? I desperately need my dose of Debbie magic! Let me know when you're free!"

My stomach grumbles a little and I realise I have missed breakfast this morning. I steal another glance out the window, where the warm sunlight dances invitingly, and on a whim, I decide to venture out and grab a bite from the café. A breath of fresh air and a dose of Charlotte's infectious positivity will surely inject some much-needed oomph into my day. And let's not forget about that pesto focaccia sandwich—I'm practically drooling at the thought.

As I step into White Cuppa House, the morning rush has subsided, leaving the café deserted with the exception of a man sat in his favourite corner, reading a hefty book. It's no wonder—everyone's out soaking up the sun. When Charlotte catches sight of me, her face lights up and she momentarily abandons her post behind the counter to greet me with a bear hug.

"Ellie, you're back!" she exclaims, releasing me from her tight embrace. "How was Manchester?"

"It was great. It was such a treat to see the whole fam and escape from…well, everything. How've things been here?"

"Oh, you know, same old, same old. I spotted Lucia again, but she was with some other bloke, so I guess it didn't work out with the hottie. That's a shame, they looked cute together."

"Maybe they're just friends?"

"Maybe," Charlotte shrugs. "Speaking of hotties, guess who graced us with his presence this morning?"

"Mh? Who?" I reply, feigning innocence.

"Mr Americano."

"Oh, did he?"

"Yes, he did. He didn't ask about you, though…" Charlotte frowns. "Did you guys talk when you…"

Under Charlotte's penetrating gaze, my cheeks ignite like a bonfire—why must I wear my emotions on my face like a neon sign?

"Ellie Irene Matthews!" she exclaims dramatically. "I know that look. Spill the beans right this instant." My stomach gives another growl that even she can hear and she seizes here opportunity. "I'll even resort to bribery. What can I get you?"

"A sandwich would be great," I confess. "But would you *lower your voice*?"

"No. Or rather, yes. I'll do even better than that, I'll be quiet and you can start talking. Now."

I join her behind the counter, watching as she expertly crafts my focaccia sandwich *à la Ellie* with an extra layer of hummus, and start telling her all about my second date—and first night—with Hugo. Charlotte's reactions range from squeals of delight to gasps of astonishment, so dramatised and perfectly timed that I feel as if I'm in a reality TV show.

"I knew it!" she yawps, causing the old man to peek up, startled by the commotion. "I sensed something was different about Hugo this morning, but I never expected *this*. Look at you go, girl! I'm beyond impressed."

She couldn't look happier if Niall Horan had just invited her to join him backstage after one of his concerts (I prefer Harry Styles, but I guess we're both quite patriotic in that regard). I give her an awkward smile, taking a hearty bite of my sandwich, unsure of how to respond to Charlotte's unbridled enthusiasm.

Don't get me wrong—I'm thrilled too—but I've been working overtime to maintain a level head and focus on more pressing matters, aka my job situation, and her boundless excitement is making it *extremely* difficult.

Just as Charlotte's relentless interrogation threatens to reach new heights, the entrance door swings open, and in glides Juliette, like a ray of human sunshine sent by the May sun itself. Her ochre bohemian dress flows around her, accompanied by the gentle jingle of golden bracelets that seem to harmonise with every step she takes. With her silver curls cascading like a crown of wisdom, and a voice tinged with a melodic French accent, she is a living, breathing work of art.

"Good morning, Charlotte," Juliette calls out. "Could I have an iced hibiscus tea, *s'il-vous-plaît*? It's scorching outside. Oh, hello there, Ellie!"

Her smile beams in my direction, and I quickly gulp down my last mouthful of focaccia, attempting to respond in kind. I simply adore Juliette—her warmth, her selflessness, and the genuine kindness that radiates from her very core. She's one of those remarkable souls who possess an incredibly grounding presence, capable of illuminating any room and making it a better place.

"Bonjour, Juliette," I finally manage to articulate after I've swallowed down the bread. "How have you been?" I lick my teeth with the tip of my tongue, for good measure.

"Not too shabby, *merci*! The shop has been keeping me quite busy lately. We have a few new volunteers, and training them has been quite the task. Charlotte mentioned you were up in Manchester? It's been ages since I've been there—my sister-in-law resides in those parts, but she often ventures down to London for work, so we rendezvous here instead of up north."

Juliette's presence alone brings a sense of tranquillity, and I can't help but feel a wave of relief wash over me. With her arrival, the spotlight shifts from my personal affairs back to the charm and energy she effortlessly exudes.

And just like that, a brilliant idea pops into my head—I can't believe I haven't thought of it before.

"Juliette, would you be interested in coming to my podcast?"

Juliette looks at me with a delightful mix of confusion and curiosity. "To your podcast, Ellie? Why on earth would you want me babbling into a microphone?" she quips, her lilting accent lending an extra touch of elegance to her words.

"I just think you're great," I reply, genuinely. "I think you are inspiring and beautiful, inside and out. I'd love nothing more than to sit down with you and listen to whatever it is you have to say! And—what if we recorded the podcast right here in the café?" I propose, turning to Charlotte. "After we've closed up shop for the day. Wouldn't that be great?"

At first, Juliette and Charlotte exchange glances that clearly scream: *"what is she on about?"* But before long, Charlotte's face lights up with excitement, her nodding becoming increasingly vigorous.

"Oh yes, that'd be great! Of course, you can record it right here. And we can even snap some Instagram-worthy photos for our social channels!" Charlotte exclaims, her enthusiasm contagious.

I shoot her an appreciative smile—she really is my best wing-woman, and Ellie's Track's number-one fan. Juliette, however, still seems unsure, pondering what she could possibly offer to captivate my listeners. But I have an eye for exceptional guests, and I'm certain that her wisdom and unwavering positivity would resonate with more than just a few.

"So...what do you say?" I press, anticipation bubbling in my voice.

"Eh *bien*... why not?" Juliette finally accepts, her smile bright and cheerful. "If you're sure. Let me give you my phone number so we can arrange a date once things calm down a bit at the shop. Speaking of which, I really ought to get back," she adds, handing me the napkin with her scribbled number. "Lovely to see you, ladies!"

With a refreshing sip of her iced tea, Juliette gracefully turns and exits the café, leaving behind the faint rustle of her flowing attire and a delightful neroli scent.

"I should probably head out too," I sigh, suddenly aware of the time. I've already spent nearly an hour at the café and duty calls. "I'll see you tomorrow?"

"Cassandra will be taking the afternoon shift with you tomorrow," Charlotte informs me. "But I've been thinking, why don't I join you for volleyball on Saturday for once?"

I raise one eyebrow in surprise. "No leg session this week?"

"I can move things around."

"Then yes, that's a great idea! Excellent. I'm sure Dan will be thrilled to see you on the court."

"Dan?" she feigns innocence.

"Oh please. Don't think I haven't noticed the way you look at him. But it's all good!" I interject before she can respond. "In fact, it's great! He's handsome, he's nice enough, and I think he's single."

"And he's a Capricorn. Which is perfect, since I'm a Virgo, and—

"Yes, exactly. Anyway, I must dash."

I give her a quick hug and make my exit, leaving her before she can drag me into more astrological considerations. Besides, she's probably already pondering the perfect attire to wear on a scorching spring day while playing volleyball and looking as attractive as possible. It's no easy feat, from my experience, but I'm confident she'll pull it off.

Once back home, I hang the laundry out to dry (thank goodness, no more wet dog smell) and settle back behind my computer. Just as I do, my phone bleeps, and I can almost hear Debbie's deep, warm voice in my head as I read her text.

"Hey, guuuuurl! It's been far too long. Yes, let's catch up next week! Are you free on Thursday? Let's grab something by the docks, like the old times—I can't wait to see you!"

A wide smile spreads across my face at the prospect of reconnecting with her and relishing in her contagious laughter echoing through

St Katherine's docks. I swiftly reply to confirm our girls' date, set another 30-minute timer, and dive back into my job hunt.

TEN

May leaves with a bang and a gloriously sunny late May bank holiday, and I end up working the weekend to earn some extra cash. Honestly, I wish I had kept a tally for the number of iced lattes we sling daily at the café. It seems like White Cuppa House is suddenly the hottest spot in town, and I don't remember seeing such snaking queues outside last summer when I was just another parched customer in need of a cold drink.

Come Monday night, Charlotte and I decide to treat ourselves with our hard-earned money—even before it graces our bank accounts, because apparently, that's how the cool kids roll. We seek solace in the comforting embrace of a chilled cinema room, ready to catch the latest *Magic Mike* movie while sipping on milkshakes. When the credits roll and the room illuminates, I honestly can't tell if I am feeling refreshed or even hotter than before.

It was a really good movie.

Over the next few days, the cruel reality of my limited wardrobe slaps me in the face repeatedly. It's an ongoing battle with my reflection in the mirror as I try to strike the perfect balance between weather-appropriate and café-friendly attire in this scorching heat. Luckily, the late afternoon brings some respite, and when the heat of the day subsides, London reclaims in my heart its throne as the best place to be.

On Thursday night at 7:35 p.m., I am perched on Tower Bridge, waiting for Debbie without an ounce of impatience in me. I'm just soaking in the breathtaking view with a mixture of awe and a pinch of cynicism, as any true Londoner would.

Below me, the grassy patch is sprinkled with tourists and locals, all basking in the elusive warmth of the setting sun. It's a proper mosaic of characters—hipsters sipping craft IPAs, families wrangling their unruly children in a queue for Flakes, and even a group of pensioners locked in an unexpectedly intense game of chess.

The atmosphere up here is electric, buzzing with laughter, chatter, and the occasional rumble of a passing double-decker bus. It's the kind of energy that makes you feel alive, like you're a small but essential part of something much grander. You can practically taste the excitement in the air, mingling with the faint scent of caramelised peanuts wafting from a street vendor nearby.

My eyes wander to the Shard again, its pyramid-shaped structure basking in the final rays of sunshine. And just like moths to a flame, tourists gather around me on the bridge, clutching their selfie sticks with wide-eyed wonder, desperate to capture the essence of

London's iconic skyline. They contort their faces into every angle, experiment with every filter, and strike pouty poses—all in the name of that perfect Instagram shot. I can't help but smile as I lean against the sturdy iron railing, fully aware that I may forever live on as a background character in countless tourist photos taken tonight.

"Well, hello there, beautiful."

I turn around at the warm, velvety voice breaking through the buzz and find Debbie, gracefully gliding towards me. She's a vision in her beige satin dress, a stunning contrast against her soft, dark skin, with her long braids swaying in the breeze. Her confidence radiates as she struts along the bridge, effortlessly navigating the flow of passers-by, who seem to instinctively part ways for her.

"Look at you, you gorgeous queen," I respond, matching her tone.

We greet each other with a brief, sticky hug, eager to escape the sun's relentless rays and find some shade with a cold drink.

Descending the stairs, we make our way towards St Katherine's docks, a charming waterfront enclave brimming with cute restaurants and pubs, and settle into *The Melusine*. It's a charming seafood restaurant that Debbie and I have dined at more than once, and definitely our go-to spot when we crave fresh air, delectable cuisine, and crafty G&Ts. A waiter guides us to our table, and as we sink into our chairs, Debbie gazes around, her eyes widening in awe.

"Ellie, have you seen these boats?" she exclaims. "They're like floating mansions! I swear they've grown bigger since the last time I was here."

I chuckle, surveying the luxurious vessels that line the docks. "Wouldn't surprise me if some of those owners have pet cobras and personal masseuses on board," I remark with a knowing nod.

Debbie joins in the game, her eyes widening dramatically. "Or if someone was held captive in the hold, screaming for help right now…"

"Whoa, that took a dark turn," I interrupt with a shiver.

She throws her head back and bursts into laughter, the sound echoing through the enclave.

Just then, a waiter arrives to take our G&T orders, and a moment later we clink our glasses together in celebration of our reunion.

"Ellie, I have to confess," Debbie begins, her voice slightly subdued, "I wasn't sure how to handle the whole situation… You know, with you being made redundant and me still working at Banders… It felt awkward."

I wave away her concerns, offering her a reassuring smile. "Oh, love, don't be silly! I understand why you might have felt that way, but there's nothing to feel awkward about. I mean, you're not the one who pushed me out the door and signed my redundancy letter, are you?" I chuckle.

"No, definitely not," she sighs, visibly relieved. "Trust me, if I had it my way, there are at least a dozen people I would've happily shown the door, but certainly not you. I'm still gutted you left."

"Aw, thanks, babe," I say, raising my glass to her. "But I'm genuinely happy for you, and you deserved that promotion. Now, enough about me. Spill the tea! How's life after the merger? Any juicy gossip?"

Debbie shrugs, appearing nonchalant about the latest developments. "Oh, you know, it's been alright. Things feel a bit strange, though. The dynamics have changed, and Mariana is driving me *nuts*—she's all over the place."

Mariana, Debbie's boss, is a petite Italian woman with short black hair and a thick accent despite the many years she's been in England. She may be smart, but she's not the best manager, often passing on her stress to Debbie and the rest of the team.

"I can imagine PR must be buzzing with the acquisition and rebranding."

"You bet," she replies with a sigh. "Not that anyone cares about Banders becoming Vonders or the new logo and all that jazz, but we have to spread the word to everyone and their brother. Speaking of which, check out our new logo."

She scrolls through her phone and shows me a sleek black capital V followed by a lowercase s and a red dot on an oval off-white background.

"Not bad," I admit.

"Yeah, it's alright. At least it's not some ugly green monstrosity. But anyway, that's the big news we have to peddle. We even have a company-wide party on Saturday to celebrate the acquisition and rebranding at the Proud Cabaret."

"The one in Embankment?" I ask, my eyes widening. "Wow, they're going all out! And knowing you, Debbie Matongo, you'll steal the spotlight in a fabulous dress."

She smiles from ear to ear. "Damn right, girl! But enough about me. What's happening in your world? Any job leads? Any hot dates? And how's it going with Amar?"

"Not much on the job front, unfortunately. And as for Amar, well, nothing new there, which is for the best. But I may have met someone… nice?"

I give her a brief account of my dates with Hugo, and by the time I'm done, Debbie's eyes are sparkling with excitement.

"Oh, Ellie, I'm thrilled for you! He sounds really into you."

"Does he? I mean… maybe, I don't know," I reply, trying to sound nonchalant, although my high-pitched voice probably betrays me. Truth is, I can't *stop* thinking about Hugo. He lingers in my mind far too often, especially during long days spent scouring job boards at home. I mean, I'm sure you can understand that it is rather hard to stay focused when my thoughts keep drifting back to what happened on the very same sofa I spent my days slouched in.

"Let's see how things unfold," I say, attempting to convince myself as much as Debbie. "But anyway, that's that. What about you? Anyone caught your eye lately?"

"Well, Emily has moved to Australia now, so I can finally move on with my life without fearing I'll bump into her at Tesco. I've been on a few app dates, but everyone there is so dull, I can't be bothered. And then… there's this guy at Vonders."

"Oooooh go on then, tell me more."

"He's quite senior, and I don't see him often because he's on a different floor and always in meetings. I don't even know his first name yet. But whenever we cross paths in the corridors, he smiles and says hi. He is very handsome, and I haven't seen any ring on his finger. So who knows? I might find out more at the party on Saturday. With the dress I'll be wearing and an unlimited tab at the bar, if there's something to explore, I'll find out right then and there."

"Cheers to that!" I exclaim, raising my glass to her before realising it's empty, and Debbie's hand shoots in the air to signal the staff.

"Excuse me, could we have the same again please?"

ELEVEN

"This is the most boring shift *ever*," Charlotte moans.

I agree. It is Sunday afternoon and here we are, trapped in the confines of the White Cuppa House. The cruel sunbeams mock me from outside the windows, tantalisingly beckoning me while I'm stuck here battling the boredom of this mind-numbing shift for the sake of a mere few, yet *much needed* extra pounds.

Even Charlotte's presence can't do much to lift my spirits. We've pretty much covered all of the topics we could think of—even the upcoming Niall Horan's concert at the Shepherd's Bush empire and how likely it is that we could get a selfie with him after the show—and she's been distractingly polishing the counter for the past twenty minutes.

Another heavy sigh escapes her lips, and we exchange a knowing look. I decide to whip up a couple of iced almond lattes, partly to keep myself busy and partly to provide us with a comforting, chilled elixir.

"Here you go," I announce, handing Charlotte her cold beverage with a flourish.

"Thanks, I owe you my sanity," she says, her eyes slightly glazed over, as if already lost in the bliss of caffeinated relief.

For a moment, we both sip our drinks silently, enjoying the meagre consolation brought by each refreshing gulp. The air hangs heavy with our collective weariness, and boy, do my legs feel heavy, too.

"I'm so sore from yesterday's game," I groan, massaging my swollen thighs with exaggerated tenderness. Note to self: invest in a good pair of compression leggings for future volleyball shenanigans in the sun.

"I'm not surprised, you put on quite the performance, my little graceful gazelle. Jumping, smashing, and all that. Very impressive."

"Oh yes, you're right. I was like a graceful gazelle, wasn't I? Except without the grace or the gazelle part. More like a flailing walrus. That's how I feel now, anyway. Stupid water retention. "But hey, I did manage to pull off a few epic saves," I add, feeling a hint of pride. "And we won. So, totally worth it. Even if today my body feels like it's been trampled by a crash of stampeding rhinos."

"You did win," Charlotte nods supportively. "It's a shame Amar wasn't there to witness it, but I'm glad I was. Trust me, the entertainment value was off the charts." I know that by that she's referring to Dan's naked torso and arms rather than my athletic performance, but whatever. "And if that can make you feel better, I too am feeling dreadful and off my game today."

"Ah, is someone nursing a hangover, perhaps?" I raise an eyebrow.

"Let's just say, deep conversations and alcoholic hydration in blistering heat don't mix well."

I let out a laugh, remembering Charlotte's valiant efforts yesterday to match Dan's drinking sip for sip during their hour-long chat after the game, only to be rewarded today with a pounding headache.

"Well, I hope your heroic efforts result in something more enjoyable than a hangover," I quip. "Have you two talked about hanging out outside of volleyball?"

"He mentioned grabbing a drink next week, so let's see if he follows through. But that'd be nice—I wouldn't mind something like you and Hugo have."

I choose not to delve into her comment, unsure of how to respond.

Hugo and I are still due to head out to the sea for the day tomorrow, but the truth is, I don't know where we stand after a week of back and forth and clashing schedules. It's starting to deflate my enthusiasm to see how difficult it is for us to meet up, even though we live so close to one another. But to be fair to him, he did warn me about his busy week with work, and although his messages have been less frequent, I can tell he's making an effort to check in regularly.

Well, except for today—it's nearing five o'clock, and I haven't heard a word from him.

Charlotte settles back onto her stool, clearly beaten and back to her moody boredom. I decide to give her a few moments of respite while she regains her energy, allowing her to savour a few more sips of the invigorating—and, dare I say, exquisite—almond iced latte I whipped up for us.

Casting a quick glance around the empty café, ensuring we're still alone, I decide to bend the rules a bit. Normally, phones are a strict no-no behind the counter during our shifts, but with no orders to prepare and the suffocating languor enveloping us, I reckon a little distraction won't hurt.

I reach into my pocket and retrieve my phone. Charlotte throws me an absent-minded glance, seemingly granting her informal approval for this brief deviation. I open Instagram and start mindlessly scrolling through an assortment of posts, reels, and stories, a virtual journey through the lives of friends and strangers alike.

Inevitably, I find myself tumbling down a rabbit hole of pandas and Jason Momoa reels, momentarily engrossed by the funny and manly videos alternating before my eyes. When I snap out of my captivated state and refresh my feed, the algorithm surprises me with Debbie's latest post from a couple of hours ago.

Goodness gracious, she looks absolutely *stunning*.

I scroll through her carefully curated shots of last night's Vonders event. Each picture showcases Debbie radiating beauty and confidence, dressed in a silky lilac cocktail dress, puffy at the top but that clings to her curves in all the right places. Her braids cascade elegantly over her shoulder, adorned with strategically placed silver rings that add a touch of whimsy. Dangling from her ears, a pair of long, delicate silver earrings glimmer under the dim lighting of the room. I can only imagine the number of heads she turned with her magnetic allure, commanding attention with her poise and captivating smile.

Our earlier conversation about her plans to seduce that handsome senior colleague comes to mind, and one thing is certain: no straight man on Earth could possibly resist this black goddess's charm. Even I can't get enough of her, and I've never been attracted to a woman before.

My curiosity is piqued as I notice the small green circle around her profile picture, showing that Debbie has shared stories solely for her "close friends". I find myself gaping at the short videos showcasing the daytime splendour of the venue, bedecked with elegant beige peonies, pristine white roses, and vibrant green foliage. Vonders' logo proudly graces every corner, a clear indication that a night to remember is about to unfold.

Debbie treats us to snapshots of the buffet, showcasing dainty petit fours being meticulously arranged by a swarm of impeccably dressed staff, and an impressive collection of prosecco bottles and glasses, ready to quench the guests' thirst. A caption playfully hints, "Something's cooking..." Yet, from what I've seen so far, that's an understatement. We did have a few good company events when I was at Banders, but nothing of this calibre.

Come night-time, Debbie continues to document her night with a classic bathroom mirror selfie and a boomerang of sparkling bubbles in a glass. Then comes another video, shot by someone else, recording Debbie expertly balancing cups of various shapes and beverages on a tray, with the caption, "Climbing up the corporate ladder one drink at a time."

"Definitely a "Close Friends" story," I mutter to myself, acknowledging the somewhat HR-issue nature of the content.

Next comes another video, capturing Debbie and her colleagues—some familiar faces, some new—joyfully tearing up the dance floor. Glasses clink in celebration as they revel under the proud gaze of Vonders' towering logo.

And then, out of nowhere, it feels as if I've been struck in the gut.

Debbie posted one final video from that night, the tone of her voice in the background hinting at the indulgence of one too many glasses. Under the caption "To new beginnings", the camera pans over the jubilant crowd surrounding her until it settles on a man standing directly in front, his glass raised to meet hers with an affectionate clink. He places his glass down on a nearby table, flashes her a bright smile, and the recording abruptly ends, leaving me stunned.

A gaping hole forms in my stomach as I process the weight of this final scene from Debbie's night. It's a smile I've seen before—a smile I would recognise in any crowd. A smile that I've felt pressed against my own lips and that's been haunting me since.

It's Hugo's.

TWELVE

"Ellie, are you okay? You look like you've just seen a ghost," Charlotte's voice echoes from a distance.

No. This can't be happening.

"Ellie?"

Instead of replying, I show her Debbie's final video. Charlotte furrows her brow, her eyes narrowing in concentration. Suddenly, her gaze widens, and she looks up from the screen.

"Is that... Hugo?" she whispers. "On your friend's Instagram? What is he doing there?"

I nod, still speechless. My heart pounds in my throat, my knees threatening to give way. If I attempt to speak, I'll either be sick or collapse on the spot.

"But there must be a reasonable explanation," Charlotte observes, swiftly regaining her composure while mine lies shattered at my feet. "Did he not mention anything about that party? Not a single word?"

"I... I think he works at Vonders," I finally manage to stammer. "I believe that's what's been keeping him so occupied this entire week, just like Debbie. And..."

It's a thought I hesitate to voice aloud. For the past five minutes, my mind has raced, piecing together fragments of the puzzle, attempting to make sense of it all. And I've reached a conclusion I'm reluctant to admit, for I don't want it to be true.

"And what?"

"I think he might be the one who signed off on the redundancies in the merger." My words stumble out, and even as I say them, I know they are true. "I think Hugo is the reason I've been let go from Banders."

***

This is a terrible idea.

It is 9:45 the next morning and I am standing before the escalators leading to Platform 3 at London Bridge station, wondering why I even got out of bed. Even the sky is watching over me in concern, looking like it could start raining any second. As for me, I *will* burst into tears if anyone else bumps into me in their rush to make it to their platform. I mean, *seriously*.

The announcement comes for the 9:53 train to Brighton, departing on time. Hugo, however, is running late, and our chances of catching it are dwindling. That is, assuming I even board this train.

After yesterday's shock, Charlotte graciously allowed me to leave work a bit early. I went straight home, only to find myself pacing the living room for most of the evening. I even had a small glass of whisky on an empty stomach, and soon enough, a gentle tipsiness enveloped me, like a snug blanket warding off the chill on a wintry day, soothing me a little.

Around 7:00 p.m., Hugo finally messaged, apologising for his prolonged silence and confirming our plans for today. He suggested meeting at 9:40 at London Bridge, and said he couldn't wait to see me again. Not knowing what else to say, I replied with a simple: "OK, sounds great!"

I have no back spine and this, right here, is my punishment. Here I stand, my beach bag clinging onto my shoulder, feeling odd and out of place. I'm on edge, and with every passing second, I'm tempted to abandon ship and run back home, or jump on any random train and never look back.

Just as the turmoil inside me reaches its peak and I am wondering if he has had the *audacity* of standing me up on top of everything else, Hugo's voice breaks through the chaos.

"Ellie!"

I spin around, and there he is—shuffling towards me, a bag hanging off his shoulder, looking like a charming disaster carrying two cups and some paper bags. He plants a little kiss on the corner of my lips, and my heart sinks a little deeper. Why does he have to be so ridiculously handsome? And how can he manage to look genuinely sweet when he's been hiding a chunky, brutal piece of truth from me?

Why?

"Sorry I'm late," he says, his smile stretching from ear to ear. "I stopped to grab us some breakfast, but the card machine had a meltdown or something. Anyway, I hope you're hungry because I have loads. I couldn't decide if you're more of a sweet or savoury breakfast person, so I got us options."

I remain speechless as conflicted feelings rise inside me. His face is breaking my heart with its adorableness, but I can't simply ignore the fact that he's been keeping secrets from me and acting like everything is fine. And I fully intend to confront him, but it's not that easy when he looks at me like that.

"Hugo," I begin, my voice trapped in my throat, "we need to…"

"Hurry, right?" Hugo interrupts, glancing nervously at the departure board. "Yes, let's get a move on."

I don't do so much as blink and he's already darting up the escalator, shooting me worried glances and urging me to follow. Reluctantly, I climb the stairs and leap onto the nearest coach, just as the doors close behind me, sealing our fate within these metal walls.

"Wow, that was close," Hugo pants, still catching his breath. "Sorry I rushed you. Should we find seats?"

We navigate through the train, and luckily, we stumble upon a square of four empty seats—one of the perks of travelling at off-peak times. In a thoughtful gesture, Hugo settles into the backward-facing window seat, leaving me with the best seating option. He places a cup of iced coffee and a bottle of water in front of me, along with a spread of breakfast options on the table between us. My god, he really *did* go to town with it. Meanwhile, I watch him, motionless and quiet, my heart pounding in my throat like a rebellious drum.

Hugo must finally notice something is up with me because his expression shifts from relaxed to concerned.

"Is everything alright? You're looking very pale. Get something down you," he says, pushing a paper bag towards me. "Have some water?"

I peer up to look him in the eyes, pulling myself together. I can't keep silent forever, but I wish we weren't sat on a train surrounded by strangers. This is neither the time nor the place for this conversation, but I feel trapped against a wall, with no escape.

"Actually, there's something I've been meaning to ask you," I muster the courage to articulate.

He falls silent, giving me a slight nod to show he's listening. I have a multitude of rehearsed questions crossing my mind, ranging from "What in the world were you doing at Vonders party last Saturday?" to "What was Debbie wearing under her lilac dress?", although that one might be slightly too confrontational.

"What have you been up to this weekend?" I compromise, keeping my voice steady and calm. "Considering how crazy busy you've been at work. Did you manage to squeeze in any fun?"

Hugo leans back in his seat, a relieved sigh escaping his lips. "Oh, it was absolute madness at work, but things should finally settle down now. We had this work event on Saturday night to celebrate the completion of a project. And yesterday... I didn't do much, honestly. I needed some rest and some TLC. What about you?"

Some TLC? From whom? I stare at him, still unsure of how to proceed. Is he genuinely oblivious to my concerns, or is he deliberately trying to evade them?

Okay, let's try again.

"Do you happen to know a Debbie Matongo?"

"Debbie who?" he responds, looking confused.

"Debbie Matongo," I repeat. As his expression remains blank, I take out my phone and run my fingers swiftly through my photo albums until I find the evidence: a screenshot from Saturday's video showing Hugo smiling at Debbie's camera.

As realisation dawns on him, Hugo utters those two simple words that hold a world of meaning.

"Ah… shit."

I can't help but agree wholeheartedly. This is a mess—an absolute mess—and he'd better have a convincing explanation for it.

But he says nothing. Silence engulfs us, and before long my mind starts racing, my worries filling the gaps in my head. Every passing second feels like an eternity. I can't bear to look at him, so I avert my gaze, fixating on the scenery outside the window.

Anything to avoid locking eyes with him, because I know I will crumble.

"I'm not sure where to start," Hugo finally speaks up, his voice laced with sincerity. "But I'll try. I'll tell you everything you want to know. And... I'm sorry."

I can't help but notice the genuine weight of remorse his words carry, and after a few seconds of hesitation, I steal a glance in his direction. Hugo's face reflects contrition, his gaze thankfully not on me but fixed on his cup of coffee as he nervously bites his lip.

I let out a deep sigh, trying to gather my thoughts.

"Let's not do this here," I suggest, finding my voice at last. "We'll talk on the beach."

The remainder of our journey is enveloped in a deafening silence. From the outside, we must appear like two strangers sharing a table on a mundane commute, just like countless others. But within, I feel a tempest of emotions brewing, threatening to burst forth. It's a constant battle—restraining the urge to explode into tears, or let anger consume me.

When we finally arrive in Brighton, Hugo awkwardly gathers our untouched, now cold breakfast. As we exit the station, he hands out our baked goods to a small group of homeless individuals who shower him with gratitude and then, silently, we make our way towards the waterfront.

As we tread upon the serene beach of Brighton, a tranquil atmosphere envelops me like a soothing balm. The seaside always is my refuge from the chaos of life. The gentle sway of the waves, the soft burble of the seashells licked by the water—it all brings a sense of calm that is hard to put into words, and hard to explain.

Growing up in Manchester, the beach was a distant dream but my rare moments by the shore in the summer always felt like a slice of heaven. And still now, many years later and in spite of my love for the city life, every time I find myself looking at the waves, gentle or crashing against the rocks, I feel home.

The sky is a bit clearer now. A soft breeze carries with it the salty tang of the sea, mingling with the inviting aroma of waffles and traditional fish and chips stalls nearby. Seagulls glide gracefully through the air, already on the lookout for an early meal, their squawks blending with the rhythmic lapping of the waves. The golden glow of the sun and the wind, a gentle touch upon my skin, feel like a caring guardian angel whispering me words of encouragement, and the sea spray leaves a delicate shimmer on my cheeks.

But amidst this idyllic tapestry, I am acutely aware of the contrast between the outward tranquillity and the melancholy that grips my guts. The laughter of couples strolling hand in hand nearby fills my heart with a lingering ache of loneliness as I glance at Hugo, a few steps ahead, his eyes fixated on the vast expanse of the sea. The pebbles beneath my feet, cool and steadfast, grounding me, stand as silent witnesses to the difficult conversation that is about to unfold.

We find a spot on a small mound of stones, away from the raucous seagulls, and we sit down uncomfortably.

"How long have you been working at Vonders?" I ask finally.

His response comes swiftly, showing his eagerness to cooperate. "A little over two years."

"And you were involved in the Banders acquisition?"

"Yes."

"So you decided who stayed and who had to go when the acquisition was signed."

My words are stinging with some sharpness I can't suppress, my cheeks suddenly flushing with anger.

"Well… yes, indirectly I did," he admits, surrendering. "We crunched numbers and identified what needed to happen for the merger to work, and that meant reshuffling teams and a few people had to go. But it's nothing personal, Ellie, it's just..."

"Oh *please*, don't give me that speech," I snap, frustration getting the better of me.

He remains quiet, probably giving me an opportunity to lash out, but when I don't, he continues, his voice soft.

"You probably don't want to hear it, but it's true. And yes, I know it sucks, but it's just a role among a list of others, and it's just how it is. I didn't remember your name was on the list. Hell, I didn't even know you back then."

"Oh trust me, I get that you deal with that all the time, and never mind if it only takes a signature for a handful of people somewhere to lose their job overnight," I snarl, trying really hard to keep my voice down even though I feel like shouting at him. "I understand the business side, the numbers, the hard choices. What *does* feel personal, though, is that at some point since we've been talking, you realised what was going on. You heard me talk about Banders, you must have put two and two together, and you said nothing. You just carried on as if there was nothing wrong, expecting me to never find out."

I turn my head to look at him. A strange expression is etched across his face, something that resembles a mixture of regret and understanding.

Or maybe that's just what I want to see. But the truth hangs heavy in the air, still waiting to be acknowledged—like a water balloon filled to the rim threatening to explode and shower us in cold water.

"I didn't know how to tell you," he admits finally, his gaze unwavering. "It kind of hit me like a ton of bricks on our first date when I realised that the designer role we made redundant must have been yours. I went to check files the next day because I couldn't stop thinking about it. But honestly, what could I have said? Would it have changed anything?"

I tilt my head, studying him carefully. "I don't know. Maybe it would have, maybe not. All I know is that right now, I'm feeling pretty stupid."

"Ellie…"

"What? Can you blame me for feeling betrayed? You've been keeping this from me for weeks—and it's not the only thing, is it?" I add before I can stop myself.

Confusion clouds Hugo's face. "What else are you referring to?"

"Why did you pretend not to know Debbie?"

There. I couldn't hold it in any longer. I know we're entering a completely different territory now, but there's no point in acting like this hasn't been on my mind at least as much as the rest of his little secrets.

And it doesn't help that I perceive a hint of frustration into his voice when he replies.

"Because I genuinely don't *know* her! We work at the same company, sure, but until Saturday, I didn't even know her first name, let alone her last name. And that video you saw? Honestly, I don't even remember it being taken. I was pretty drunk by then. Come on, Ellie."

I avert my gaze, muttering under my breath, "Well, you two certainly seemed cosy."

"I'm... not sure what to say," he continues, his voice taking on an unfamiliar chill, like a sudden gust of winter wind—or is it just the distortion of my anxious mind playing tricks on me? "What are you implying?"

I'm convinced he knows exactly what I'm implying, but he places the ball squarely in my court, daring me to address the elephant in the room—the complexities of dating in this day and age, and the implications that come with it. Sure, we never said anything about being exclusive. We only slept together once. But does everything really have to be so scripted nowadays?

I suppose it does, yes. I've already had my fair share of burns, scars still healing from the Elliott fiasco. You'd think I'd learned my lesson, not to expect too much from someone I barely know. Not to *assume* things, but also not to get too excited too quickly, or worry at the first hurdle. And yet here I am, doing all of these things at once, sad and deflated and feeling like a complete fool.

Anger swells within me, threatening to overflow, and I quickly rise to my feet, taking a few hasty steps away to hide the tears welling up in my eyes.

These past months have been an outrageous whirlwind, a tumultuous rollercoaster ride of emotions like I had never experienced before. And honestly, I think I deserve a bit of positive karma at this point. I should ask Charlotte what my birth chart says, but I think I am due for a big sun in my seventh house or something.

"Ellie, will you please *explain*?" Hugo pleads behind me, but I ignore him, still too agitated and upset to bear to face him.

Not that I *particularly* enjoy crying my eyes out and dwelling on the past, but you know—sometimes it's all you have. Sometimes, you just need to allow yourself to feel miserable for a little while, and then when you're done crying, you dust yourself off and you move on. You move forward. Onwards and upwards.

As far as I can remember, I've always imagined myself having a family and kids, a job that I love, and a house by the sea. At 32 years old, I have none of these things. But as things unfolded, dating naturally took a backseat, relegated to a place lower than my annual dental check-up and my not-so-meticulous plant care routines. I accepted it as a necessary hiatus, with the conviction—or maybe the naïve hope—that things would fall into place eventually, and love would find me when I am in the right place for it. I've been focusing on myself and the balancing act that is my life, and sure, I'm still kind of surviving rather than thriving, but with a somewhat healed heart and a temporary job that I grew to love, I thought I was on the right path.

So—why?

Why did Hugo choose this exact moment to disrupt my precariously reconstructed world, where the stitches are still fresh and the wounds threaten to reopen with the slightest pressure applied to it? Was this just another curveball flung my way, a reminder not to lose focus and to stay true to what truly matters to me?

Was he never meant to stick around?

Suddenly, it hits me like a caffeine buzz after too many espressos. The answer lies right there, amidst all these swirling questions tormenting my mind. Whatever this is, the cocktail of anxiety and insecurity and loneliness it stirs within me is not worth it.

I can't add this extra layer of stress to my already unstable life. I can't afford to squander precious energy and time on something as uncertain as dating.

I need to feel in control of something, and that means I can't let someone else in until I feel truly secure within myself.

I just can't.

I pivot to face Hugo, summoning every ounce of courage I possess, inhaling deeply as the seconds tick away, each breath a countdown to the moment I alter the course of our connection.

"I can't do this," I finally say, my voice steady, my tone, resolved, not belying any of the turmoil wreaking havoc inside me. "I'm sorry, this was a mistake."

"What was a mistake? What are you talking about?"

"This. Us. Whatever this is—*was*. I can't do it. It's too much stress, and I can't do it."

Hugo's eyes are fixated on me, the expression on his face undecipherable. I wonder if he's figuring out how to respond, but I don't let him any time to. Now that I've opened the gates, I can't close them again. It's either that, or I'll do something even more embarrassing, like, I don't know. Scream at the top of my lungs or angrily throw pebbles in the water.

"I can't keep up with the high and lows. My life is already a work in progress and I just don't know how to fit this piece into the messy puzzle I have on my hands. Spending time with you has been... great. Like a breath of fresh air. It felt nice, and it felt simple. But now all of a sudden it's like I'm being dragged even deeper underwater and I'm struggling to break the surface."

I pause to catch my breath, allowing my words to linger in the air. My heart thrums within my chest, my flushed cheeks betraying my nerves. The distant memory of Hugo's radiant smile to Debbie comes back to me, and my knees threaten to collapse under me. "I can't be playing the guessing game of what this is or what this means," I falter. "I don't want to feel anxious wondering why the hell you're drinking prosecco with one of the most *gorgeous* women I know on Saturday night and then buying me breakfast on Monday morning. I don't know what to think, or how to behave around you, but all I know is that I can't continue like this."

"Ellie..." His voice is surprisingly calm and soothing, as if trying to coax me out of my own tangled thoughts. "I'm sorry I didn't tell you about Vonders. Really, I am. And I'm not entirely sure what you think you saw on that video with Debbie, but... don't you think that you're maybe... overthinking everything a little bit?"

"I know I am." A wave of frustration and vulnerability crashes over me, and I feel an irrepressible urge to pour out my insecurities and fears in a rush of words. "I know I shouldn't have these expectations, and it's unfair to burden you with the weight of my uncertainties. But here's the thing—I can't help it. I'm feeling insecure as hell, and it's turning me into someone I don't recognise. It's not the person I strive to be. It's like I'm at my lowest point, and yet, you *somehow* still manage to like me. But can you see the irony here, Hugo? How can I date you now, when I'm at rock bottom and resenting you for playing a part in my life literally falling apart nine months ago?"

Hugo's body stiffens as I blurt out this last part, and I bite my tongue in remorse. Shit. That was too far.

"I see," he says finally as he rises from his spot on the pebbles, his voice cold as ice. My heart drops, regret settling in like an unwelcome guest.

"Hugo, I'm sorry, I didn't mean— "

But he raises a hand, cutting me off, and I understand our conversation has come to an end. Silence falls between us, the sound of crashing waves providing a dramatic backdrop to the moment. My throat tightens, a mix of pins and needles coursing through my body. I can't bear to look at him directly, so I cast my gaze downwards. Waiting. Several agonising seconds pass, stretching into eternity, before I finally gather the courage to raise my gaze. But it's too late.

I'm met with the sight of his retreating figure and the quiet screeching of his steps on the pebbles, his hair tousled by the wind, as he walks away.

THIRTEEN

I don't think this could have gone any worse.

Standing alone on the beach, replaying the conversation that just unfolded again and again, I ponder the aftermath of my decision.

Hugo's hurt face is still etched on my retina. I mean, I can't blame him for walking away—even I cringe at the burning memory of my own spiteful words. But although I could have packaged it better, I know deep down I meant everything I said. This is what I wanted— all cards on the table, and a clean break, with no looking back.

But then, why does it hurt so much?

Feeling agitated, I start walking, my feet taking charge while my brain is still overheating from the surplus of heightened emotions I've had to deal with over the past few days. On autopilot, I stroll along the shore, my mind filled with a thousand bubbling thoughts, bobbing like the lightest seashells tossed about by crashing waves.

I make my way towards the marina, passing by Brighton Pier. My gaze traces the length of the pier, from the lively arcades to the majestic Ferris wheel standing tall against the horizon. The spirited crowds and joyous ambiance wrap me in a bittersweet embrace of memories from past visits. It's as if I'm observing a vibrant carnival from afar, where the echoes of laughter and excitement reach my ears.

The marina teems with boats of all shapes and sizes, instantly bringing to mind Debbie and our recent conversation over dinner. I know that the mature and sensible thing to do would be to call her to finish piecing together the puzzle I hastily assembled—and eventually, I will. But for now, I indulge in dwelling on my circumstances, allowing myself a moment longer of self-pity and contemplation. Maybe nothing truly happened between her and Hugo at the party—perhaps her mysterious man was someone entirely different altogether. Maybe that was an unfair accusation on my part.

But still, I firmly believe that ending things with Hugo today and turning over a new leaf in this tempestuous chapter of my life was the right choice to make. It's better this way, for everyone involved—I just need a few days for things to settle down a little bit. At least, that's what I tell myself.

Hours pass as I wander along the shoreline, finding a bit of comfort in the rhythmic embrace of the waves, until eventually the misty air begins to chill me and I decide it's time to head back.

Once I reach home, I waste no time in summoning the heartening powers of a pad Thai to my doorstep. While my saviour—a delivery driver called Rasha with a 4.7-star rating on Deliveroo—makes his way to my flat, I surrender to a blissful soak in a warm bath, allowing the soothing water to wash away the remnants of the day.

Then, clad in my comfiest attire and with the aroma of my dinner filling the room, I settle onto the sofa, snug and somewhat content. I spend the rest of the evening browsing through panda reels, eating spoonfuls of cookie dough ice cream and watching *Notting Hill* for the millionth time. In this moment, I relate more than ever to William Thacker's feelings of foolishness when he lets Anna slip away. I don't know yet what my happy ending looks like, but until then at least I don't have to deal with a flatmate as eccentric as Spike.

And if I ever have to leave this beautiful flat and share my space with a stranger, surely there are plenty of fantastic people in London that definitely do *not* mistake mayonnaise for yoghurt.

Right?

Needless to say, when I pick up the afternoon shift alongside Cassandra the following day, I am still feeling pretty down. The air between us hangs heavy with silence, but I prefer it this way. For once, I am actually relieved that Charlotte isn't around today, as I'm not sure I could handle reliving the entire Hugo conversation and the ensuing depressing rest of my Sunday. Caught up in my own thoughts, I do my best to keep up with the customers' orders and navigate the day.

"*Bonjour, Mesdemoiselles*! Could I have a chai latte please?"

Juliette and her *joie de vivre* have just entered the café, catching both Cassandra and me by surprise. I'm not used to seeing her on my afternoon shifts as she rarely stops by outside of her morning routine. I take a split second too long to regain my composure and smile back at her, but it's enough for her to take notice of the sombre expression etched across my face a mere moment ago.

"Are you alright my darling?" she asks as Cassandra takes her payment and I get into motion to prepare her drink. "You look like you lost your favourite macaron. Is something the matter?"

I let out a half-hearted chuckle—Juliette always has the most endearing idioms. "I'm fine, I was just…lost in thoughts."

"Are you sure? I know you Brits are too polite to really speak your mind, but if anyone can hear it, it would be me! Maybe you need to take a page of the French and be a bit more blunt every now and again. Now, I won't pry, but I can see there is something troubling you, my lovely, and I wish I could help you."

My eyes well up instantly—gosh, I am oversensitive these days. Juliette is standing a few feet away from me, with a relaxed smile and a welcoming attitude, and once again I am moved by her natural glow.

"It's just that...I'm questioning everything. I'm finding it hard to remember who I am and who I want to be. And don't get me wrong, I love working here, but I feel like I'm losing myself sometimes, you know? "

Juliette leans against the counter, her voice filled with empathy. "Oh, my darling, I hear you. Life can be tricky. But you know, *ma belle*, the right opportunities come along when you expect them the least."

I sigh, frothy up some milk absent-mindedly. "I know," I say when the loud noise of the steamer subsides. "I guess I'm just a bit deflated right now. Like... this foam," I add, frowning as I notice the sad excuse for a foam heart on top of Juliette's cup.

"I think you used the oat milk," Cassandra comments, flatly. I grunt, realising she is right, and make a move to discard the drink in the sink but Juliette reaches across the counter, gently grasping my wrist to stop me.

"It's all good, I'll take this one! I should really watch my dairy intake anyway."I offer her a weak smile, gratefully, and place the cup in front of her. "Don't be too hard on yourself, my love," she continues reassuringly. I think you need a bit of fun. Why don't we grab dinner tonight? My nephew was here last weekend and brought along a *trove* of lovely French delicacies but I would hate to keep it all to myself. Charcuterie and cheese are meant to be shared, don't you agree?"

"That sounds lovely," I reply, genuinely. "And maybe we could squeeze the podcast recording as well?"

Just as I say that, I realise in horror it's been nearly three weeks already since I released the last episode, just before I went to Manchester. How did I let myself get so distracted? I used to be so consistent with it, even when I worked at my full-time job, I still managed to post an episode every other week or so.

And I love Ellie's Track! I love everything about it—the people I meet, the editing itself. And now, it's not only one of the last remaining ties I have to my previous life, it's also part of my portfolio that hopefully will get me a job soon. I can't let it slip. Thankfully, my evening schedule is clear for the rest of the week, so if we record the session tonight, I could have the new episode ready by Friday.

"Well,*bien sûr, pourquoi pas*! " Juliette replies and I let out a sigh of relief. "French food, laughter, good conversation, and a glass of wine can work wonders—as long as we make sure not to speak with our mouths full, I suppose."

"Fantastic!" I exclaim, smiling from ear to ear. "Let me just double-check with Charlotte to make sure we can still use this space, and if it's all fine let's say 8:00 p.m. here tonight? I'll text you to confirm!"

"*Parfait*! I'm looking forward to it. See you tonight then—*Au revoir*!"

***

"Oh my *god* Juliette, this is incredible!"

I snap a picture of the exquisite spread of cheese, wine, bread, butter, and charcuterie laid out before us. The two microphones are visible in the background, their red LEDs blinking already. I send the photo to Charlotte to post on the café's socials and as she replies with a thumb up emoji, Juliette and I can finally dig into our scrumptious feast.

She *really* has outdone herself with the French delicacies. With each bite, I can't help but shower her with praise, and when I repeat for the fourth time how fantastic this salted butter is, she offers to give me her nephew's number.

"He's a cheesemonger in Normandy," she explains, pride clearly visible in her eyes. "Quite the talent, isn't he? Oh, and did I mention he's single? He even appeared on a French TV show called *L'Amour Est Dans Le Pré*. It's a show where farmers find their soul mates," she explains when she sees the confusion on my face. "But alas, no such luck for him. Maybe he needs to think even more outside the box—for all we know, his soul mate might be a barista."

I suppress a chuckle, trying not to burst into laughter. "Well, I haven't come across that show before, but I'm not certain I'm ready for it." I grab another cracker and a slice of brie with a bit of apricot jam. "I am, however, *more than happy* to be his pen pal if it means I can get a steady supply of this divine cheese every now and then."

Juliette lets out a laugh, delicately dabbing her lips with a napkin. "You're absolutely right, darling. French nibbles are simply the best. That's why I love Boro Bistro—it's a taste of home whenever I'm feeling nostalgic."

"Oh yes, I forgot to tell you I went there recently!" I exclaim. "It was so good. And the place is very charming too, with all the fairy lights…it was a really nice dinner."

A little pang of bittersweet memories tugs at my heart as I remember my first date with Hugo. It feels like it was just yesterday when we sat at the restaurant for hours. The moment we shared on the roof of his previous apartment, lost in contemplation of the

Shard, is still etched in my mind. And then, our first kiss outside my front door…

Except that what *did* happen yesterday, is that I chased him away.

Juliette, blissfully unaware of my suddenly clouded thoughts, continues with her cheerful banter. "It truly is, isn't it? I tried to pry the secret recipe for their *mousse au chocolat* out of them, but no luck. Anyway, shall we get started?"

I nod, grateful for the change of subject. "The microphones are already rolling," I inform her. "I like to capture everything on record because unplanned tangents often make for the most entertaining moments. It helps with the editing and it adds a bit of rawness to the final episode."

"Aha! It's like B-Roll, but for sound snippets," Juliette muses.

"Yes, exactly like that, actually," I reply, genuinely impressed by her quick grasp of the concept. "How did you become so knowledgeable about video production?"

"My sister-in-law—well, she's my ex-husband's sister, but we remain close—works in the industry. She's part of a short film production company based in Manchester. Whenever we go on holiday together, she always receives calls from work. She's a busy woman, Emma. And very important in her company. But after each conversation, she fills me in on the matters so that I don't feel left out, and so over time, I've picked up quite a bit myself."

"A production company in Manchester?" I echo, racking my brain for familiarity. "Could it be Mancunia Motion Pictures?"

"*Oui*, that's the one!" Juliette nods, her eyes sparkling. "Do you know them?"

Is this a real question? " Yes! I really, really liked some of the movies they made. They even won an award last year for the best British silent short movie for *Passagonia*—I mean, it was only right they did. That film is incredible—have you seen it? And didn't they handle the latest Anna Mangler perfume video too?"

"Oh my, Ellie, you're a true fan!" Juliette chuckles. "Emma would be very pleased to hear you speak like that! She always says the company doesn't get enough recognition for the work they do but it's good to see that it doesn't go unnoticed."

"Well...that's my industry as well," I explain. "Before I joined White Cuppa House, I was a motion designer in an agency in London. I studied in Nottingham and Mancunia Motion Pictures is quite prominent up north. One of our teachers worked there, actually—a Mr Dobson?"

"James Dobson! Yes, I do recall Emma speaking to him on the phone. Ah, what a small world! Perhaps I should introduce you to Emma. I don't know if they're looking for anyone at the moment, but I'm certain the two of you would hit it off anyway. You'd have plenty to talk about."

I practically gasp in excitement."You would do that?"

"Of course!" she replies, like it's the most natural thing in the world. "Emma is a remarkable woman. When my husband and I parted ways after twelve years, I couldn't imagine my life without her any more. Trust me, you'll see why when you meet her. She's strong, driven, and fiercely loyal—a lot like you, Ellie."

I blush at her praise—I'm not very good with compliments.

"She will be in London for a three-day congress next week," Juliette continues, "and we're planning to have lunch at *Applebee's Fish* on Friday. Would you like to join us?"

"I... Yes! I'd be delighted! Are you sure Emma won't mind?"

"*Mais non, pas de problème!*" Juliette waves off my concerns with a dismissive gesture. "It will be splendid. I have a great feeling about this."

She leans to top up our glasses and I help myself to more bread and cheese. The twist in my day has taken me from feeling sad and deflated to hopeful once again. I don't know what will come out of this meeting with Emma, but it is by far my best shot at getting my foot back in the film industry in a very long time.

I come back to my senses, suddenly realising that I have hijacked the conversation with my career shenanigans. Rather embarrassed, I swallow my mouthful and clear my throat.

"Welcome back to another episode of Ellie's Track. Today, I'd like to introduce you to my guest and dear friend Juliette Mocquin—and I can't tell you how happy I am that she's agreed to join us."

FOURTEEN

I haven't quite lost track of dates and times, but one thing I know for sure: my weekends lately are not exactly *weekending*. It's Saturday morning, and after what seems like an eternity of editing, I am happy at last with the final cut for the episode. Sinking into the plush embrace of my sofa, I can sense the heat radiating from the cushions, reminding me that we've officially entered the scorching realm of mid-June. Oh, the joys of summer, when the temperature skyrockets like a faulty thermometer on a hot air balloon.

Don't get me wrong, I absolutely love London at this time of the year, but this level of heat feels like an overenthusiastic, sticky hug from a distant relative that you'd like to see more often, but less intensely.

Still, the sauna-like humidity in my flat is nothing compared to the stuffy air outside. My blinds remain stubbornly closed, partially attempting to shield me from the relentless sun, partially representing my denial about the upcoming volleyball game in the park and the searing rays of the sun that'll be singeing my skin, turning me into a piece of crispy pork crackling.

The idea of sweating profusely while lunging in the sand for a ball doesn't exactly scream "fun in the sun" to me. It's more like "baking in a human-sized oven", topped with a generous sprinkle of chafing. Not my notion of a good time.

At the mere thought of it, I realise how parched I am, and a tantalising craving for an iced latte sneaks its way into my consciousness. But venturing out into the sweltering inferno close to lunchtime, even for just a few minutes, is not on my agenda today.

No, thank you.

I shuffle my way into the kitchen, conducting a thorough investigation of the fridge and cupboards in search of the necessary ingredients to concoct a less-than-stellar homemade iced latte. It won't be a five-star experience, but hopefully, it'll scratch the itch.

Pouring simmering instant coffee over a handful of ice cubes, I add a dash of almond milk and stir my drink with a metal straw. My heart skips a beat as I notice the delicate beads of condensation immediately forming on the glass. And the first, glorious sip tastes like heaven. It's funny how coffee, hot or cold, always manages to make the world seem a little brighter.

Ambling back into the living room, my hands clutching at my glass of frosty bliss, I notice the leaves of my green babies drooping dramatically. Oh God, they look even thirstier than me.

Setting my drink down on the table, I grab the watering can and make my way back to the kitchen to fill it up. As I pour the water into their pots, the soil greedily absorbs it, leaving me feeling like a terrible plant mum. With my misting bottle in hand, I generously spray my monstera and my philodendron, imagining their weary leaves sighing with relief.

"Hang in there, buddies," I murmur, leaning in closer as if they can understand my words of encouragement. "I know exactly how you feel."

In my mind, I can hear Mam's voice complaining about the unbearable heat back in Manchester—she would never survive in London, that's for sure. I picture her cooling herself with a handheld fan, her face flushed and her hair sticking to her sweaty temples. With a wistful smile, I make a mental note to call her tomorrow when she and Dad visit Nan for the traditional Sunday roast.

When I return my attention to my latte, the ice has already melted away, and with a few gulps, the whole drink is gone, too. Now what? I need a practical solution to combat this relentless heat wave—it's not even July yet! A fan would do the trick, I suppose. It's not exactly the stuff of legends, but it beats turning into a puddle on my sofa. And it's not like I can afford to rack up a sky-high water bill by taking cold showers all day, either.

With a lazy swipe of my phone, I delve into the depths of Amazon. Predictably, most of the cheaper options are already sold out, and the featured ones seem more like luxury items than necessities. The choices are overwhelming—tower fans, desk fans, fans in every shape and size imaginable. After careful consideration, I settle on a sleek, inexpensive one that promises to be powerful. Plus, it boasts a guaranteed three-day delivery. Only three more days of sweaty misery before my salvation arrives.

With the order placed and a fleeting sense of victory washing over me, a notification rudely interrupts my moment of triumph. It's a bank alert, informing me that I've just gone into overdraft.

Great.

I release a frustrated groan and, with a few more swipes, transfer a couple hundred pounds from my savings account. I won't receive my pay for another two weeks, which means…

Which means that I can stay in denial and pretend that I still have time to figure things out. Because I don't. With the rest of my savings and my shifts at the café, I'm going to need to make some drastic changes quick if I don't want to be homeless in…three months? Yep, that's it, three months.

And by drastic changes, I essentially mean find a job right this second (and perfectly on cue, another *ping* in my mailbox tells me it's not happening), or finally admit to myself that I have no choice but to move out of my beloved flat, my haven, my cosy home in the middle of London, and swap it either for an overcrowded student flat share in Shoreditch, or a small studio flat way outside of London.

The mere thought of it sends shivers down my spine. I've been chasing my tail and buried my head in the sand, but now this is it. I have run out of time, and run out of money, and I need to face the consequences.

With a resigned sigh, I open my personal email and bring up my landlady's address. The least I can do at this point is to tell her where I'm at and ask her if she would be okay with me starting to look for a new tenant to take over my lease. I've never caused any issues in the flat, looking after it as if it were my own, and hopefully she accepts to let me look for a replacement as a back-up plan. That way, we've covered all bases and I don't need to hand her in my notice *just* yet.

Just in case my luck finally turns around.

***

Three hours later, after a mere twenty-five minutes of volleyball, the sweltering heat becomes too much and we collectively wave our white flags, unanimously deciding to call it a day.

Seeking a less hostile environment, we find refuge under the shade of a few trees and gather beneath its branches, feeling the cool grass beneath us. A few brave soldiers volunteer to make a supermarket run and fetch us drinks and ice creams to quench our parched souls. The rest of us settle in and while we await the return of our heroes, I bring Charlotte up to speed on my financial predicament and the decision I made. Gosh, between my dwelling on the Brighton disaster with Hugo and now this, she must be tired of all of my lamentations this week. But as the true friend she is, she listens to me attentively, nodding and humming in all the right places.

"That's the right thing to do," she says immediately when I finish my update, and her unwavering support fills my aching heart with a fizzy warmth. "It's ideal, all things considered. That way, you're still buying yourself some time in case something comes up. And it will! All it takes is one job—and you're meeting with Juliette and Emma next week, right? So who knows? Maybe this is it. This might be the opportunity you've been looking for."

"That's true," I concede, "but even if a job does come up, it'll be based in Manchester. So I would still need to move out of my flat since, you know, it'd be a four-hour commute or something. I'd have to leave London and everything behind."

"Well, maybe this wouldn't be such a bad thing. I mean, yes, I'll be *gutted* if you leave, but no one says it has to be forever, and I'm sure your parents would be happy to have you back. Have you spoken to them yet?"

"Not yet. I'll call them tomorrow and tell them."

"It's going to be fine."

The rest of the group returns bearing bags of refreshing drinks and treats, and Dan, Amar, and a charming girl named Lia settle down beside us.

"What did we miss?" Dan asks as they start unpacking the snacks.

"Ellie may or may not move back to Manchester in a few months," Charlotte replies immediately.

"Really?"

"Yes, but…"

"Nothing is confirmed yet, but either way, it's going to be fine and we're supporting her. Can I have a Cornetto?" she asks as Dan rummages through the plastic bags.

"Of course we're supporting you," Amar nods, and I raise my eyebrows in surprise. "You're getting a bit too good at volleyball, I can't have anyone threaten to challenge me for my seat on the throne like that." I jab his arm in protest, but can't help but smile widely at him. "No but seriously, Ellie, you'll be fine. And just because you leave London, that doesn't mean we won't see each other any more. You can always come back and visit us, or we'll come and visit you."

Charlotte nods with unwavering support. "Absolutely! And who's to say you couldn't have a hybrid work arrangement? You're always welcome to come and stay with me. We'll find you a cosy corner in White Cuppa House, and you can work from there. It'll be like you never left!"

Her smile radiates hope, and I choose not to point out that it is *impossible* to cram an entire motion designer workstation into my suitcase, nor that it really wouldn't fit in the café's decor.

It's the thought that counts.

"Let's see how things go," I simply say.

"And about your flat—maybe Lia could hold it for you?" Amar suggests, turning to Lia who widens her eyes at him. "Didn't you say the other day you wanted to move out from your parents' house?"

"I—yes, I mean... I wouldn't want to step on anyone's feet," she fumbles, her words tumbling out in a rush. "It's true, I've been thinking about moving out, but I haven't properly started looking yet..." Lia glances at Amar, who's still grinning like a Cheshire cat, clearly triumphant. "But if you're looking for someone, I'd really like to..."

"This is grand!" Charlotte chimes in, her face lighting up with delight. "See? No problems, only solutions. Now you can relax and focus on that interview, and you can tell your parents tomorrow that there *may* be a possibility of you moving back home, but that you have everything under control."

I force a small smile, not yet entirely convinced but grateful for their enthusiasm and will to help. "Thank you guys. And... yes, that could work, actually. Lia, if my landlady is okay with the arrangement you could come around some time and have a look at the flat, see if you like it?"

"Cool, I'd love that!" she agrees, visibly delighted.

We exchange smiles and I notice how Amar, too, gazes fondly at her as he hands her a Magnum. Meanwhile, Dan, busy opening bottles of beer for everyone (with an alcohol-free option for Amar and Lia), steals a glance at Charlotte, who's savouring her ice cream a little too enthusiastically for public display.

Oh, boy.

Charlotte glances back at him, innocent (not), and I can see the tell-tale blush creeping up his neck. And let me just say, it's refreshing to witness someone else wearing their emotions on their sleeve for a change. Dan shifts slightly, his hand gripping his beer bottle tighter as he takes a long swig to cool himself down.

Bless him.

The budding romances (or summer flings, at least) are palpable around me, and before I can stop myself, my mind shifts back to Hugo, and how I wish I could change the course of things. But then again, it would just make my decision of leaving London even harder.

Maybe this is all for the best, after all, and I'm hoping that in time I'll realise it, and wonder what on Earth took me so long.

FIFTEEN

It comes as no surprise that Applebee's Fish is absolutely packed when Juliette, Emma, and I arrive there at 12:30 p.m. on this furnace-like Friday. The restaurant is buzzing with the typical TGIF energy as locals and tourists converge to indulge in the delicious seafood and fish delights it has to offer. The tantalising aroma of sizzling dishes wafts through the air, teasing my senses.

If it weren't for the healthy amount of stress coursing through my veins at the thought of this important "business lunch", as Charlotte rightfully called it, I'm pretty sure my stomach would audibly growl in anticipation.

But right now, it's all tangled up in a knot of nerves.

We're escorted to a table on the outdoor dining terrace, situated just across the street from Borough Market. Grateful for the refreshing water the waiter offers us, we profusely thank him as we settle into our seats and begin perusing the menu.

"Oh God, I have no clue what to order," Emma declares, her eyes darting so quickly across the menu that I wonder if she's done a speed-reading course. I looked into those a while ago, it's an actual thing, but ironically in order to increase your reading speed, you first have to read *a lot* of stuff to train your brain. And honestly, who has time for that in the first place? "There's so much to choose from!"

That's an understatement. Applebee's menu is *extensive*, to say the least. Each dish description sounds absolutely divine, rendering my decision-making process more difficult than I anticipated. I need a minute to collect myself, and I'm not just talking about the food. I need my nerves to calm down so I can put my best foot forward in front of Emma. I need a distraction.

And as I often do when I'm nervous and I'm playing for time, I resort to bad jokes.

"On a scale from fish and chips to mussels and garlic bread, how adventurous are you feeling today, Juliette?" I ask with a mock-serious expression.

Juliette chuckles. "Ah, Ellie, you forget who you're talking to. A Frenchwoman like me would never dream of indulging in mussels in London. They're meant to be savoured by the sea, preferably prepared and cleaned with one's own hands while sipping a glass of chardonnay. And as for the British obsession with garlic bread, it puzzles me. They're called *moules-frites* for a reason."

"Oh dear, sounds like I've struck a chord. Now I'm afraid of what you might think of me if I dare to order them."

"Oh, Ellie, don't be silly. I could never think any less of you. Of course, you should order them if you're tempted. As for me, I believe I'll go with the salmon tagliatelle. And what about you, Emma?"

Emma closes the menu with a decisive gesture. "I think I'll opt for the chowder," she says confidently, "And a Sauvignon Blanc to accompany it. Should we share a bottle?"

Emma McLane is an elegant woman in her late forties, with a radiant smile and sharp green eyes. If her choice of clothes today is anything to go by, this woman has impeccable taste. On this sweltering hot day, she's somehow managed to maintain her professional poise while embracing the need for breathability — something I found most difficult achieving myself.

But Emma looks perfectly at ease in her chic knee-length linen dress in a soft shade of pastel blue, superbly complementing her rosy complexion and blond hair elegantly tied in a low ponytail. The dress hugs her figure flawlessly, with its sleeveless design and modest V-neckline adding a touch of femininity without compromising her overall elegance. Resting against the back of the empty seat next to her is a matching blazer, crafted from the same breathable fabric. Though she won't need it for several more hours, Juliette mentioned that Emma has a busy afternoon and evening of important meetings ahead and the air does still get pretty chilly at night.

As for her shoes—*heavens*. Despite the heat, Emma manages to appear comfortable in her high-heeled crisp white sandals, and that itself forces my utmost respect. Truly, her effortless grace needs to be acknowledged, as does her choice of equally refined accessories, with delicate silver jewellery adorning her wrists and fingers.

Emma has naturally caught the attention of more than one onlooker since our arrival, but she carries herself with a quiet confidence that suggests she's accustomed to such admiration. It's not just her attire that sets her apart; it's her poise, her presence, and her perfect posture—shoulders back, head held high—radiating the self-assurance that comes with a successful career and years of experience of the business world.

In preparation for today, I did a bit of online research about Emma and found myself feeling somewhat embarrassed as I read about her numerous personal and professional achievements that I had no idea about.

She started from the very bottom of the ladder as a runner and climbed her way up, owing her current position to no one but herself, her wit, her determination, and her skills. Her years in the film industry have moulded her into the extremely successful and influential woman she is today, with a keen eye for talent and an innate understanding of both the intricate politics of this world and the latest creative trends.

She also shares a strong bond with her twin brother, whom she started a charity with after his daughter was diagnosed with myopathy. Together, they organise fundraising events and campaigns, including an annual White-Collar boxing training camp culminating in a night of boxing fights at Depot Mayfield in Manchester.

So I hope I can be forgiven for walking into this meeting thoroughly intimidated and, frankly, a little flustered by all of Emma's achievements. However, as the minutes go by, I find myself feeling less and less nervous, gradually becoming accustomed to her presence. She has a kind and pleasant nature, and her subtle Geordie accent adds a touch of warmth and familiarity to her words. As we sit at the table, engrossed in lively conversation amidst the vibrant atmosphere of Applebee's Fish, I can't help but be completely captivated by her.

The waiter takes our order and swiftly returns with a bowl of olives and a bottle of wine. We clink our glasses in unison, and as I take a sip of the Sauvignon Blanc Emma chose for the table, my taste buds come alive, tingling with the wine's refreshing notes of citrus and gooseberry.

Is there anything this woman isn't good at?

"Delicious," Juliette comments approvingly, setting her glass back on the table. "But we'll have to watch ourselves with this wine. It's so refreshing, but in this heat? If I'm not careful, next thing I know, I might just doze off in my plate of pasta!"

Emma and I burst into laughter, unable to resist Juliette's endearing authenticity. Her remark reminds me of the infamous mishap with Aunt Agnes's spaghetti Bolognese from my childhood, and I contemplate for a second whether sharing that story would be appropriate for today's company.

"So, Ellie, Juliette told me about your podcast," Emma jumps right into the conversation, pulling me back from my brief moment of reflection. A surge of warmth floods my cheeks, though, to be fair, it could also be the combination of the heat and the couple sips of wine finally working their way through my system. "She played it for me this morning, I found it most interesting."

A shy smile tugs at the corners of my lips at Emma's compliment. "Juliette was an absolute delight to have as a guest," I respond, shooting my friend a grateful glance. "We've received an abundance of comments from listeners raving about your energy and that charming accent of yours, Juliette. Not that it surprises me one bit, of course."

Juliette's face beams with a mix of humility and pleasure. "*Ooh là là,*" she exclaims in her delightful French accent. "You're making me blush, stop it!"

"I've listened to a few other episodes, too," Emma continues. "I must say, they're all really good. And the number of downloads is quite impressive, especially without any marketing backing."

A surge of pride washes over me, mingled with a sense of accomplishment. The countless hours poured into each episode, the dedication to creating something meaningful—it's all starting to pay off.

"Thank you," I reply, feeling a touch sheepish for not having a more composed response to such praise. "When I started the podcast, it was simply a way for me to connect with people. I think more and more listeners joined in each month because they resonated with the stories of my guests. I still don't feel like I can take much credit for its success, though. I couldn't do it without my guests."

Emma shakes her head, her elegant poise unwavering. "I disagree. You absolutely can, and you should," she insists. "Sure, having interesting and likeable guests is important, but you need good editing and an engaging host to do them justice. That's also what makes a podcast worth listening, and what builds listenership."

"Well...thank you," I repeat, my cheeks positively burning me now. "I suppose the podcast naturally took shape around the formats and energy that resonate with me. The first few episodes were even released with visual recordings, but then some guests preferred not to be on camera, so I dropped this format. It was probably for the best anyway—work was getting a bit hectic and editing for the podcast was consuming most of my free time and becoming a bit draining."

"It's so important to know your boundaries and stand your ground," she nods in agreement. "And knowing where to compromise, too. In our industry, it's easy to get swept away, trying to do too many things at once. It takes discernment and a strong mind to find the sweet spot between doing enough and chasing something that will never truly satisfy you. And I'll be honest, working endless hours isn't the solution, in my opinion—you need time out to let creative juices flow and find inspiration to keep the machine going."

She takes another sip of her wine, her confidence and presence radiating more intensely than the midday sun. Next to me, Juliette remains silent, herself, too, basking in Emma's aura.

"So, tell me, Ellie, what *is it* that you truly love doing?" she enquires.

I pause, allowing her question to sink in.

It's been ten months since I left my previous career, embarking on this uncertain journey of finding my next steps. During this time, there have been moments of hope, tears, bursts of energy and creativity, as well as bouts of despair, loneliness, and self-doubt. But throughout it all, my dreams and aspirations have remained my guiding light, leading me back to the same conclusion time and time again.

"I love creating things that move people," I reply earnestly. "The entire creative process, from start to finish, is what brings me joy. It gives me purpose. There's nothing quite like diving headfirst into a project I wholeheartedly believe in and pouring my heart and soul into it. And then, when the time is right, sharing it with the world. Seeing a project through and releasing it to the world, that's what gives me the buzz."

Emma's eyes lock onto mine, a smile lighting up her face.

"You care," she states, and her voice carries a surprising tint—almost like pride. "And that is invaluable. It's rare to find in our industry, where too many people are motivated by the wrong reasons. Egos often get in the way of delivering truly outstanding work. Ellie, I'd love to see your portfolio if you have one. At Mancunia Motion Pictures, there will always be a place for someone with the right attitude and skill set."

With a graceful motion, Emma retrieves a business card from her bright orange clutch bag and slides it across the table, causing my heart to skip a beat.

"Do you have a portfolio I could look at?"

"Y-yes, of course!" I stutter, clutching the card in my hands as if it were the Holy Grail itself. "I'll send you the link this afternoon."

She gives a satisfied nod just as the waiter approaches us again. With excitement taking over and untying the anxious knot in my stomach, I suddenly realise how ravenous I am. I wish I had followed Juliette's recommendation and ordered a side of chunky chips to accompany my dish of mussels, but I suppose I can always grab a slice of banana bread on the way back.

I deserve to treat myself.

The rest of the lunch goes swimmingly well, with Juliette and Emma catching up like the old friends they are, and ensuring I am included in their conversation. I relax a little after our encouraging chat, happily engaging in their debates, gossip, and jokes. As they casually mention Julian, Emma's brother and Juliette's ex-husband, I am amazed by her positive attitude towards their relationship. She was able to let go of the past and embrace her new life with open arms—maybe that's the secret to happiness and peace.

My plate finished, I excuse myself and head inside the restaurant to find the bathroom. As I step inside, I freeze in my tracks, my heart pounding in my chest. There, by the till, stands a familiar face.

"Elliott?" I blurt out.

"Oh wow, Ellie!" he exclaims, his eyes widening with surprise. He opens his arms in a friendly and inviting way, and I step into his warm embrace. For a moment, it's as if time stands still, and I find myself lingering in this hug longer than I probably should. My heart flutters a little, the familiarity of his cologne bringing back a flood of memories—shared laughter, late-night conversations, and the way he used to hold me.

He pulls back slightly to look into my eyes. "You look good," he says, his voice soft and sincere. "It's so good to see you. Sorry, give me one moment." He turns his attention back to the staff to settle his bill, and I stand there awkwardly, unable to tear my gaze away from him.

It's been over a year since we last saw each other, and although we didn't part on bad terms, I chose a clear separation, with no animosity but deciding not to pretend to remain friends. For a long time, I dreaded bumping into him in London, knowing how small the city can feel at times. And now that it's finally happened, I'm struck by this strange, unexpected feeling. Almost like… *relief*?

It's as if a different version of him stands before me today. He still exudes the same warmth and confidence that I loved about him, but his shorter hair and the notable weight loss transform him into a person I no longer recognise from the memories I've carried. With this slenderer figure, noticeable even in his face and hands, he's not the man I used to know and who still lives in my head.

"Sorry," he repeats as he puts his wallet away. "What are you doing here?"

"I'm on a…business lunch," I reply, my words slightly hesitant, but deciding now is not the time for a lengthy and detailed explanation of today's logistics. "And what about you?"

"My parents are in London for a few days, so I took them out for lunch," he answers, gesturing towards two smiling figures in the corner of the room.

Returning their smiles politely, I wonder if they might recognise me from the pictures their son showed them when we were dating. Life truly works in mysterious ways. What were the odds of bumping into Elliott *today*, of all days, while he's out with his mum and dad, when the *meeting-the-parents* conversation was one of the catalysts for our break-up? And yet, I feel no resentment or anger—just genuine happiness to see him, and a sincere hope that he is doing well. Is this what closure feels like?

"I'd better get back…" Elliott says, his words trailing off. "We should grab coffee sometime, catch up?"

"Sure!" I respond, but we both know we won't. With a final smile and a shy nod, he heads back to his parents and I continue my way to the bathroom. By the time I return to our table, our coffees have arrived, and Elliott and his parents have already left.

Juliette's eyes sparkle with curiosity. "Did you bump into a friend?"

"Not exactly a friend," I confess, my smile tinged with nostalgia. "Just…someone I used to know. It was nice to see him again."

With our coffees finished and the bill finally settled (I practically had to wrestle it away from Emma's hands and insist on splitting it three ways), I say my goodbyes to Juliette and Emma and start making my way home while they head off for a leisurely stroll along Southbank.

And as if the universe was determined to send a message today, my phone pings with a text and my heart skips a beat as I see Debbie's name on the screen.

"Hey girl! How is it going? I'm having birthday drinks next Thursday at The Folly, nothing big but I'd love you to come if you can make it! There'll be a few people from Banders/Vonders too. Hope to see you there — reservation is from 7:30! xxx"

A hand of guilt grips me as I think about the last time we met and the great evening we had by the docks. I let my jealousy and my own insecurities get in the way of our friendship, and I never followed up after we met to ask her how everything went with this launch party she had worked so hard for.

Come to think of it, because I was so shell-shocked by her stories and the vision of Hugo at the party. I didn't even leave the usual fire/drooling emojis on the stunning pictures that she posted. I'm a terrible friend.

Seizing my chance to redeem myself for my shortcomings of the past few weeks, I hastily type a reply (*"Of course I'll be there!! Can't wait to celebrate you!"* with fire emojis and a birthday cake) and make a mental note to find her the perfect card and the perfect gift. Maybe some long, bright earrings—she adores them, and they always superbly highlight her slender neck.

Of course, there is a small chance that *he* will be there too, with Debbie swooning over him. That could prove...interesting. If something did happen between them and Hugo chose to lie about it, I know from experience that the Debbie Matongo won't hold back. There will be TMI and vivid details, guaranteed.

But then again, avoiding her simply out of fear for the truth that might hurt me won't do any good. I've made my decision and I need to live with it, and whatever may or may not have happened between them is irrelevant. Chances are I won't stay in London for much longer anyway, and I refuse to squander it on "what ifs" and regrets.

SIXTEEN

I spend the rest of the day in a dazed state, feeling disconnected from the world around me.

I'm feeling positively exhausted, but from the moment I set foot in my flat, far from the state of torpor I was expecting to sprawl in, a wild, unshakeable antsiness creeps upon me.

I fire off an email to Emma, attaching the link to my portfolio and hoping against hope that this umpteenth email won't be met by the same silent fate as countless ones before. Then, incapable to tame the whirlwinds of thoughts swirling in my mind, I decide to head to the gym.

And while an intense leg workout might not have been the smartest choice after a few glasses of wine and a hefty lunch, it does wonders in distracting me from thoughts of Elliott, Debbie, and my moving back to Manchester, with or without this job at Mancunia Motion Pictures that I'm so desperate for.

Lost in my semi-conscious state, I hardly even noticed Raf approaching, trying to make small talk and suggesting we share the hip thrust machine that I'm using. He looked somewhat deflated as

I casually waved him off, but another interaction with an ex is simply the last thing I need to deal with today.

As evening descends, I decide to treat myself to a relaxing bath and give Charlotte a call. Balancing my phone precariously against my ear, I pour fragrant bath salts into the water, creating a soothing oasis in the midst of my racing thoughts.

"Hey, girl," I greet her, the warm water enveloping me in a cocoon of comfort as I slide into the bath. "How was your day? Is now a good time to chat?"

"Hey you!" Charlotte's voice rings through the line. "Just getting off the tube. So, tell me! How did it all go?"

I launch into a rapid-fire retelling of my day, attempting to do justice to the events while avoiding reliving every single moment. As I recount the business lunch (this really was an appropriate name for it), the unexpected encounter with Elliott, Debbie's text and even the amusing Raf incident, I can hear Charlotte's panting on the other end of the line. That means she's reached her apartment after climbing up four flights of steep stairs, and sure enough, a second later, I can hear keys jingling in the background followed by a soft thump as she drops onto her bed.

"Well, fuck me, what a day you've had," she concludes, and I think this is a fair and accurate statement."But it all sounds pretty positive, right?"

"Yes, cautiously positive," I reply, treading carefully. "At least, it's the most promising lead I've had in weeks, if not months. So, here's to hoping."

"Exactly. You go girl. And what about Hugo?"

"What *about* Hugo?"

"Well, don't you think he'll be at Debbie's thing?"

"I— I haven't thought about," I lie. "Okay, I *have* thought about it, but what am I supposed to do? I can't *not* go to Debbie's thing, she's my friend and she's done nothing wrong."

"Well, can't you text him to find out?"

"*Text*—No! Are you serious?! What am I supposed to say? "*Hey, remember me, Ellie? We dated for a hot minute but then I completely lost the plot and ruined everything. Anyway, I just wanted to ask again if yes or no you are having a thing with this bombshell at your work because I'm invited to her birthday drinks next week and I'd like to prepare mentally if I am to see you there.*"

"Something like that, yes. Except you *didn't* ruin everything, it takes two to tango and he didn't dance too well either."

"I'm not texting him," and the categorical tone in my voice must be quite convincing, because Charlotte doesn't push it further." Anyway. How was your day?"

"Long and boring, as usual when you're not around," Charlotte sighs. "But not too shabby, I suppose. Annndddd hopefully the day is about to get better because I have a date tonight."

"What! With whom? Dan?! How is this the first time I'm hearing of it?"

"Steady on, tiger! Yes, with Dan," Charlotte replies. "And you're only finding out now because he asked me this afternoon."

"Finally! He took his sweet time."

"I know, right? He sent me a text, asking if I fancied meeting up tonight, and so, of course, I played it cool by responding immediately with a 'yes, what time and where should we meet?'"

I burst into laughter, imagining Charlotte's gleeful expression upon receiving that text. "I see!" I reply, still chuckling. "So, what's the plan?"

"I'm not entirely sure yet. He suggested we meet outside The Nightjar in Old Street at 8:00 p.m. So I need to get ready and start overthinking what to wear. Do you think it'll still be warm by 2:00 a.m. or should I grab a jacket?"

"The Nightjar?" I raise an eyebrow, intrigued. "So I shouldn't be surprised if neither of you make an appearance at volleyball tomorrow?"

"No, I wouldn't count on it. Anyway, sorry love, but I have to dash. But yay on the job front, I'm thrilled for you!"

"Thanks! Have a smashing time tonight, and don't forget to send me a picture of your outfit! And no jacket needed," I add. "If it gets cold, he'd better lend you his."

"Gotcha. Bye!"

I put the phone down on the floor and sink deeper into the bath, trying my best not to dive right back into the whirlwind of thoughts that have been following me all afternoon. After a few minutes, I can finally feel my mind drift off and both my extenuated brain and sore muscles relax in the warm water's embrace.

***

Monday morning arrives with a bustling energy at the café. With the longer, sunny days, everyone seems to be a bit more motivated to get up and start their day, and the morning rush arrives a good fifteen minutes earlier than in the winter days. I contemplate this thought as it crosses my mind, realising just how much I've come to learn about our clients' habits and how White Cuppa House and its warm community has grown on me. Even if this was always meant to be ephemeral, I will miss working at this place when I leave.

Seizing the opportunity of a short respite, I quiz Charlotte on her weekend. I tried to call her yesterday but she was having a rather rough day. Between whimpers and groans, she explained that she went from a terrible hangover to an even worse first day of her period, and that she would rather die than come into work tomorrow. And yet here she is—not the best she's ever looked, but ploughing through bravely.

"So how was your date with Dan?" I ask.

"He's a dick." I stay quiet at that short yet unequivocal statement, waiting for her to provide more details and brush the full picture. "He was nice at first and we both were feeling good and happily drunk, but then he started losing it a little bit. He kept insisting that we go back to mine and then he even flirted with another girl barely half his age at the club, right in front of me."

"He did *what*?!" I interject, aghast. I mean, I don't know Dan very well and I did think it was a bit *cheap* of him to invite Charlotte out last minute, but that's another level of shitty behaviour that even I didn't see coming.

"Yeah, I wasn't impressed. So I ordered a Uber and I left him there. I have no idea how much longer he stayed or whom he left with and frankly, I don't care. I was just glad to get into bed. Alone."

"Oh Charlotte, I'm sorry."

"Oh no, I'm grand," she shrugs. "At least now I know he's not worth it and I'll stop obsessing over him. He's not even a good kisser anyway, so I doubt he would have been much better in bed." I would normally rebuff that kind of blanket statement, but given the circumstances, fair enough. Dan's behaviour is screaming fragile masculinity, if you ask me. "What about you? What did you get up to this weekend?"

"Not much," I respond, "I've mostly been Marie Kondo-ing my flat in preparation for the visits and the move. I've thrown away some old papers and a bunch of electric cables and chargers I don't need, and I've put some clothes up for sale on Vinted."

"That's a good start," she nods.

"It's all about sparking joy, you know?"

"*Bonjour, Mesdemoiselles!*" Juliette greets us as she walks up to the counter. She's wearing a beautiful emerald blouse and a denim skirt. I swear she must have worked in fashion in a previous life—or maybe it just comes naturally to all French women. "How are my favourite baristas today?"

Charlotte and I exchange knowing glances before I respond with a bright smile, "Always better when we see you, Madame."

Juliette smiles brightly, placing her hand on her heart.

"You're too sweet. Oh it was *magnifique,* Ellie. Emma and I spent some time in Hampstead Heath, I even managed to convince her to borrow one of my swimsuits and dip in the pond! It was marvellous, and so refreshing. Ah, thank you, Ellie," she says with a graceful nod as I hand her an iced hibiscus tea—my treat, of course. A lifetime of warm and iced beverages on my tab is the least I can do to thank her for introducing me to Emma.

She leans against the counter, her eyes ablaze with anticipation. "You know, you left quite an impression on Emma on Friday—not just during lunch, but with your work as well. I think she was genuinely impressed by your portfolio. I didn't grasp all the technical details, but she mentioned something about a showreel and bionic motion graphics? She kept saying how this is the calibre of work she wants to see from her team. She's back in Manchester now but I have no doubt that you'll be hearing from her very soon."

"Really?" I exclaim, feeling my heart leap with joy within my chest. "Juliette, I can't express my gratitude enough for introducing me to Emma. The possibility of working at Mancunia Motion Pictures, after all the time I've spent searching for a job, is simply unbelievable. And it's all thanks to you," I add earnestly.

She brushes off my gratitude with a graceful smile. "Oh, don't mention it, love. This is entirely your doing—and you're already thanking me!" she adds, pointing at her cup. "You have an unwavering drive and immense talent, which, of course, Emma recognised immediately. They won't be wasted on her. I wouldn't be surprised if she was drafting an offer for you as we speak."

"Ellie, this is monumental!" Charlotte chimes in, her excitement matching mine. "Now you can return to Manchester not just because you need to, but knowing that this is the perfect career move for you as well."

She's absolutely right. If things play out the way Juliette seems to think, it would be a game changer. The thought of returning to Manchester with a purpose and a bright future fills me with excitement. I can imagine finding a cosy flat in Salford Quays or Castlefield, navigating the streets in my very own little car. And I would definitely fill the space with a copious amount of fresh new houseplants. I will look after them better, this time. New job, new place, new me—new leafy babies.

Interrupting my feverish thread of thoughts and our excited chatter, a customer waiting behind the counter clears his throat pointedly, reminding us of our duties. Charlotte swiftly offers her apologies and tends to him, taking his payment while I prepare his order (a double espresso and a croissant), and our professional dance resumes.

Juliette takes her leave, and I wave her goodbye as Charlotte nudges the next customer forward with a cheerful prompt: "Next, please!"

"An Americano, please."

I nearly jump out of my skin at the sound of the familiar voice. I turn around to face Hugo, who stands just a few feet away, his gaze fixed on me with an enigmatic expression.

Charlotte throws me a side glance, unsure how to handle the situation. She mentioned he popped by a couple times since we broke up, but I haven't seen him since our heated exchange in Brighton. Unless he's been actively avoiding me (which I would understand, to be honest), I suppose it was only a matter of time until we bump into each other again.

I take a moment to gather myself, plastering a polite smile on my face. "Coming right up," I respond smoothly, my voice thankfully betraying none of the turmoil swirling within me. As I prepare his drink, my hands move on autopilot, my mind hyper-aware of his proximity. The sound of the card reader behind me signals his payment, and I feel him shuffling closer to make way for the next customer. I can practically feel his gaze lingering on me, causing a flush to creep up my neck.

I carefully place the lid on his Americano and turn around to face him. I'm trying really hard not to stare, but *god*, he really is so handsome. It's just *not fair*.

I hand him his coffee and our fingers brush fleetingly, sparking a surge of electricity through me.

"Thank you," he murmurs, taking a step back but coming to a halt again, his reluctance to leave clearly visible on his face.

Our eyes lock, and for a second I forget all of our thorny history. Lost in the depths of his blue eyes, I feel a vulnerable flutter in my chest—the kind of sensation you get in dreams when you find out that your crush miraculously likes you back. All I can think of is how I got so lucky to become one with this man for the space of one night, and how, *how on Earth* I could be so stupid to throw it all away.

"So, you're leaving?"

And just like that, the spell is broken. This is not a dream, and while I am very much talking to my crush, our time together has come and gone already. Besides, the café is getting busier and I really should pull myself together.

Except Hugo is still standing there, his whole attention fixated on me. "I am, yes," I reply finally, the words reluctantly stumbling out of my mouth. "I've decided to move back to Manchester." My throat feels dry, my heart is pounding in my chest. A little voice inside me wants to blurt out, "Just kidding! Ha ha." But instead, I just stand still and silent, awaiting his response.

"That's...a surprise. But...I don't know, good for you, I hope?" His words betray his conflicted emotions, mirroring my own. He's treading carefully, as if waiting for my confirmation that it is indeed good news and he should be happy for me.

"Yes, it's for the best," I say decidedly.

I hope he accepts my words at face value, and doesn't delve deeper into the complexities of my decision. My confident façade wavers slightly, uncertain how long I can maintain it. My gaze shifts briefly to the growing line of customers behind him. If we continue like that, today might earn the title of the worst customer experience at

White Cuppa House. Charlotte shoots me a knowing glance, sharing the same concern but reluctant to interrupt our exchange.

"Good, good... So...maybe we could go out for dinner before you go?"

Before I can stop myself, my eyebrows rise in surprise. *Did I hear that right?*

"Dinner?"

"Yes? Or if you prefer maybe we could go for a wa—"

"No, no, dinner sounds good," I continue hastily, my voice much higher than I'd like it to be. I was not expecting that—*at all*. When things ended with Elliott, for a while I hoped he would turn around and realise he'd made a mistake, but days turned into weeks, and weeks turned into months, and I had to accept that the phone call I was expecting would never come, and that he had, in fact, moved on. You live and you learn, as Nan always says, and after the way things played out with Hugo, I had no reason to believe it would be different this time.

And yet, he just asked me out for dinner. Me. *Moi.* So—could it be? Could it be that I made the mistake, but he's giving me a second chance?

No, Ellie, *come on*. He's just being a reasonable adult and offering an amicable send-off dinner before I go. And that's already a lot more than I've learned to expect from men in London.

"Great—I'll make a reservation. Does Thursday night work?"

Well, this is becoming ridiculous now. Did he really say Thursday? I frown, not sure how to navigate the answer. "I can't do Thursday night. It's…" I hesitate. "It's Debbie's birthday? She's having drinks to celebrate. She said a few colleagues are coming too, so I figured… maybe I'd see you there," my voice falters with the last bit, and though I try to keep a neutral face, my cheeks are starting to feel pretty warm.

Gosh, this is awkward.

Awkward, awkward, awkward.

Understanding dawns on Hugo's face and he pauses before responding. "No, I haven't been invited, I'm afraid," he says causally. "I haven't spoken to Debbie again since the event, actually. But tell her happy birthday for me."

Why am I feeling so many butterflies in my stomach, all of a sudden? It's quite silly, actually, how happy that makes me. It still doesn't mean anything.

Actually, what it *does* mean, is that I was wrong about Debbie and him having a thing, which probably only makes me look even more hysterical in Hugo's eyes. So there is really no reason to feel all giddy and warm inside.

The butterflies need to *calm the fuck down*.

"I could do Friday?" I suggest.

"Can't do Friday, I'm heading to Ireland right after work—you know the holidays I told you about?"

"Oh grand! Where in Ireland are you going? Do you need any recommendations or—never mind, sorry," Charlotte backtracks hastily when she catches sight of the warning glare in my eyes and turns her attention to the milk steamer and starts thoroughly cleaning its plunger with her kitchen towel.

I mean, I love her, *but read the room, Charlotte.*

"How about tonight?

"Tonight works."

"Perfect then. 7:00? I'll text you a place."

He suddenly seems to become aware of the cup he's been holding all this time and takes a large sip of it, and I can only stare at him, unable to move or speak. With a bright smile and a nod, he turns around, and I swear the flutters of the butterflies in my stomach get so loud that the whole café must hear them.

SEVENTEEN

As Hugo walks away, I release a breath I didn't realise I was holding. I'm suddenly feeling quite light-headed but resist the urge to sit down and turn my attention back to the line of customers waiting to be served. Charlotte has been holding the fort the best she could but my slacking has resulted in a rather long queue of growingly impatient patrons, and I really need to pick up the pace.

"Good morning, sir," I greet our next patron. He's crossed his arms across his chest and tucked in his newspaper under them, and has been shifting his weight impatiently from one leg to the other. Uh-oh. "Sorry about the wait. What can I get you?"

For the next fifteen minutes, Charlotte and I work diligently behind the counter, exchanging only the bare minimum of words to catch up on the backlog of orders (which I take full responsibility for—I owe Charlotte a big glass of wine and a 'best-co-worker' sash).

The hustle and bustle of the café provide a welcome distraction, allowing me to focus on the rhythmic motions of crafting our customers' drinks. But despite the busy atmosphere, I can't shake off the whirlwind of emotions swirling inside me. The encounter with Hugo left me feeling both elated and off-kilter, and when the line of customers finally subsides, a sudden bout of dizziness creeps onto me.

"Are you okay?" Charlotte asks, concern lacing her voice.

I force a weak smile. "Yes, all good. Just need a minute."

She isn't buying it. "You need to sit down, and a glass of water," she counters with an authority in her voice that I don't often hear. I do as I'm told and sink onto the nearest stool while she fetches me a glass of cold water. I gulp it down gratefully under her scrutinising stare, the cool liquid bringing me back to my senses. Charlotte doesn't rush me; she waits patiently until I start to regain my bearings. But when she's satisfied that I'm not on the verge of collapsing, she can't hold it in any longer.

"So…what was *that*?!"

She's obviously referring to my conversation with Hugo, but I really don't know the answer to that question. "I'm not sure," I admit. "But I think we're going for dinner tonight?"

"Uh-huh?" Charlotte nods, not even trying to hide her disbelief.

"And, as it turns out, he and Debbie are not dating."

"Uh-huh."

Her eyebrows arch into her forehead as a smirk creeps up on her lips as she reads between the lines. "It's not like *that*," feeling weirdly defensive. He knows I'm leaving," I add quickly, because it feels like we both need reminded of it. "So it's not a big deal. It's *just* dinner."

"Sure. Yes, you tell yourself that. But just in case, wear your best underwear tonight," she deadpans.

"Charlotte!"

"What? Don't look at me like that! You'll thank me tomorrow."

"I'm not working tomorrow," I reply, deciding to ignore her last comment.

"I know that, but you'd better give me a call and tell me how your da—how your friendly, *platonic* dinner went," she backtracks when she catches the look in my eyes. "What have you got planned for tomorrow anyway, anything exciting?"

"Nothing exciting, no. The usual job search, I also need to find a birthday gift for Debbie, and then more cleaning and clearing my flat because Lia is coming to see it in the evening."

"Are you still searching for jobs in London, or…?"

"A little bit," I admit. "I mean, if something catches my eyes, I go for it, but I've pretty much tried all of the agencies now. I'm mostly looking in the Manchester area, see what's out there."

"Well, hopefully you hear from Emma soon," Charlotte says encouragingly, "and maybe it'll be easier to find a job up north once you've moved back, as well."

"Yes, probably."

Keen to make up for my previous lack of productivity, I stay behind the counter after the end of my shift, and it's almost 2:00 p.m. when Charlotte sends me home with a focaccia sandwich and a poppy seed muffin.

"Shoo! Take a nap, have a shower, and make sure you shave. And call me tomorrow!" she adds as I step outside, ostensibly rolling my eyes for good measure but granting her a grateful smile.

Without the distraction of the café, the afternoon drags, and I glance at my phone more often than I should, my whole body on high alert and going on override waiting for Hugo's text which still fails to arrive.

Fully aware there is no way I'll be able to fall asleep, I decide to swap the nap prescribed by Charlotte for a bubble bath. Making sure that my phone is in reach, I slide into the warm water, resting my head against the bathtub pillow, and try to relax.

I must have dozed off in the end and slept for a while, because when the ringtone on my phone jolts me awake, almost all the bubbles have gone and the water is practically lukewarm around me. I feel a pang in my gut as I see Hugo's name flashing on my screen, and with a very wet slide off my finger, I pick up his call.

"Hello?"

"Hey Ellie, sorry it took me so long to call."

I pull my phone away from my ear, careful not to drop it into the bath—it's almost 6:00 p.m. *Shit.* "No problem," I reply, thrusting myself up into a sitting position.

"The thing is, I tried to make a reservation for tonight, but all the places I called are fully booked."

My heart sinks at his words, disappointment engulfing me like a wet towel. "Ah, that's a shame," I say, deflated.

"Yeah, it is. We could still try our luck for a walk in, or I was thinking…maybe I could cook?"

I blink. Cook dinner? What, for me—for us? I can't tell if that's resolutely friendly or definitely re-entering the dating territory. My experiences would tend to hint at the latter, but I suppose friends cook together too? I mean, I cook for Charlotte all the time, so why would it be any different? Just because we used to date doesn't mean we—

"Ellie?"

"Yes! Sorry, I—I thought I heard someone at the door." That's a terrible excuse but it'll have to do. "Yes, that sounds good."

"Perfect, I'll send you the address. I need a couple of hours to cook and tidy up the flat because my flatmate took off on holiday yesterday and apparently didn't feel compelled to take care of his chores before he left. So now it's all on me. Dickhead." There's a pause and a deep breath on the line, and I take a distracted glance at my hairy legs. "Anyway, are you okay to come for 8:00?"

"Yes, 8:00 is fine. "My toes peer up above the bath water, and I notice my scaled nail polish. When's the last time I had a pedicure? "Eight is *great*. Can I bring anything?"

"Nope, I got it. Alright, I'd better get going if we want to eat at a decent time. I'll see you soon."

He hangs up and a second later my screen lights up again with his address. He does live very close (it's barely a twenty minute walk from mine), which leaves me plenty of time to get ready.

I pull the bathtub plug and while the water starts to drain, I grab my shaving cream and my callus remover. As I start applying the cream on my legs, I can practically hear Charlotte's voice ringing in smug tones in my head.

"Just in case."

***

"Here you go."

I take the glass of wine Hugo is presenting me and take a sip while he returns to preparing his apparently famous and top-secret salad dressing. He's been all mysterious about it and said he can't divulge his grandmother's family recipe, but he's already checked with me that I'm not allergic to walnuts and I can definitely smell some mustard from here, so I kind of know what to expect.

"No peeking," he says jokingly as he notices me staring at him, and I look away with a smile. He proceeds to tossing lettuce leaves and bell peppers inside the bowl, and I glance around me to take in the space.

Hugo lives in a stunning converted flat in Shad Thames with a flatmate called Andy who seems to be rather the messy type. It's the kind of place I can only dream of ever living in, a unique blend of rustic charm and modern sophistication permeating the space.

The living room is an eclectic mix of old and new, carefully curated to create a space that feels both contemporary and timeless. Fashionably vintage, the exposed brick walls hint at the building's industrial past. The bricks, weathered and worn, carry stories of days gone by, and contrast beautifully with the sleek and contemporary furniture. Soft, earthy tones dominate the decor, with shades of warm browns, tans, and beiges harmoniously blending together. A mixture of warm wooden furniture and plush cushions create a cosy ambiance, and a sandalwood candle is burning on the coffee table, its scent mingling with the smell of the homemade pizzas baking in the oven.

There's a large bookcase against one wall, filled with an eclectic mix of books and old vinyl records. The vintage record player sits atop a rustic wooden side table in a corner of the room and is playing Amy Winehouse's best tunes (my pick). On the shelves, I spy a few well-loved novels and a fair number of non-fiction books too, mostly travel guides and a couple of biographies from athletes I've only vaguely heard of.

"You don't have any houseplants."

"We used to, but I wasn't great with the watering schedule, and Andy… well, let's say that I have to pick my battles with him, and getting him to do his cleaning shores in the flat is already enough of a hassle. Don't," he cuts when he sees the smirk tugging at my lips. "Don't get me started. Okay, I think the pizzas are ready. Do you want to grab a seat?"

He nudges me towards the living area. I lay down my glass on the table before me and sit on a chair (comfortable faux leather, *nice*) while he brings over his *salade du chef* and the pizzas we made together.

"I've never had artichoke hearts on a pizza but I can see how that works," I nod in appreciation.

"Yeah? That's my grandmother's secret recipe, everyone always think it's weird until they try it."

"Another secret family recipe uh? How many do you have?"

"Well, that's pretty much it to be honest. After tonight, you've seen them all."

"Does that mean I'm part of the family then?"

A weird expression flashes on his face and I bite my lip, immediately regretting my tongue-in-cheek remark. Not able to think of something else to say, I shove another mouthful of salad in my mouth (delicious, by the way) and hope that he'll forgive my getting carried away and change the topic.

"So, how's life? And…when are you moving?"

Wow, okay, maybe some more small-talk first? What is it with everyone ignoring the basic rules of British communication today? "I'm not sure yet. But soon, I think. I might stay for the rest of the summer, but then I'm going."

"Have you found a job yet?"

"Maybe, I'm waiting to hear back. But even if this one doesn't work out, I'm sure I'll find something else."

"Yes, definitely," he says encouragingly. "But fingers crossed, anyway. Let me know how it goes."

I nod awkwardly. "Thanks. I will." He responds with a small but warm smile and reaches for the bottle to top up our glasses. In contrast with his apparent ease and composure, a growing feeling of unease tugs at my stomach, like a nagging sense of guilt and suddenly I can't hold it in any more.

"I'm sorry about what happened," I blurt out.

"Ellie…"

"No, Hugo, I really am sorry. I wasn't fair to you—about anything. About the job, about Debbie… I ruined it. And now I'm going away and it doesn't matter any more, but I want you to know it. I'm really, really sorry, and I wish I could take it back."

"I'm sorry too," he mutters, his voice soft, his eyes locking into mine. "I should have been honest with you from the start, and none of this would have happened. Well… maybe you would have wanted nothing to do with me," he says with an ironic chuckle. "But at least you could have decided for yourself what you wanted. And as for Debbie…"

"No, that one is hundred percent on me. I jumped to conclusions and I had no right to come at you like that."

He smiles. "Okay, yes. You can take the full blame for that one." I can't help but let out a little laugh, and as I do so, I can feel my shoulders relax and relief wash all over my body. This truce calling is going beyond my expectations—like, white flags everywhere, and I have a sudden vision of fireworks in the sky and a lovers-to-best friend kind of twist to our story.

"I should have called you," he clears his throat, and under the table I have to pinch my leg to make sure this is not a trick of my imagination. *Ouch.* "At first I was pretty mad, to be honest…" he sighs, looking for words, and I'm staying perfectly quiet because I wouldn't be able to speak if I tried. "But then I tried to put myself in your shoes and see where you were coming from, and I think I understand now. I understand that none of it was really my fault, but also I didn't really do anything to help the situation either. "

"I—I'm sorry, I don't know what to say," I admit. "But this means more than you can imagine, Hugo, and—"

"I'm sorry it took me so long," he continues, and I swear I am having the hardest time to contain the rush of emotions within me. "I just wasn't exactly sure… what to say, or how much space to give you. I would have reached out eventually, I promise," he adds, his tone pressing, and I believe him. "But when I heard you were leaving, I just…I just had to see you again. To say this."

He falls silent and as I watch him watch me and wait for a reaction, I panic. "Well, you are officially forgiven—or whatever," I say solemnly, raising my glass to him in possibly the most embarrassing toast I ever made.

He chuckles slightly as my face heats in embarrassment. "Come here," he says as he gets off his chair and opens his arms towards me. I get up too and not so much walk as lunge into his arms, wrapping my own around his waist as he closes his embrace around me.

I rest my face against his chest, my eyes closing in bliss, and I can feel the soft thumps of his heart against my cheek. His torso rises and falls rhythmically as he breathes, and as if following a metronome marking the pace, I can sense my own breathing becoming one with his. Unable to stop myself, I squeeze him tighter, not ready quite yet to break away from him and let this moment end.

As if he read my mind, Hugo loosens his embrace and my eyes almost start prickling in disappointment when one of his arms leaves my back. But a second later, I feel a warm touch on my cheek and a gentle tug at my chin, and I look up to see Hugo looking intensely at me. His sea-blue eyes are glaring with the same flame that's burning in my chest and spreading rapidly to my whole body like wildfire. His gaze travels to my lips and a second later, the world disappears.

The doubts, the mistakes of the past, the misunderstandings between us—they're all shattered to the ground as our lips meet again. His fingers run through my hair and as I cup his hand with mine, he pulls me towards him. The next second, my toes are off the floor and he gently sits me on the table so that my head is level with his.

We break apart for a short moment, catching our breaths and a glimpse at each other. His desire is etched on his face, radiating from his every pore, as he must sense mine is too. And then suddenly, as if my ragged breath was fanning the flames of our lust, his fervour intensifies and I realise his excitement is lava bubbling under the surface, making his body shiver in anticipation.

His caresses turn to grips and I gasp as his tongue runs down my neck and along my collarbone, and then back up to find my mouth. I bite his perfect lips, and then I bite them again, and our kiss deepens and my longing for him becomes so intense I could cry. It's like no time has passed since the last time he was mine, my body remembering every inch of his, as if I've known him all my life. Except this time, Hugo wants to take me down a different path.

With a strong grip, he brings my writs together and holds them firmly against my chest with one hand, while his other hand travels down my stomach, my thighs, and up again underneath my skirt. He tugs at my underwear, his fingers slipping into it, and let out a faint hiccup of pleasure as his fingertips find me. My hands still pressed against my chest, wilfully trapped in his clutch, I arch my back, panting, my body rocking electrically with every stroke, and I abandon myself to this frenzy under his fiery glare.

It's like we're suspended in the moment, embracing in a parallel universe where no past or future exist and only the now matters. There are no seconds or minutes or hours, no quantifiable measure, and we're lost in time, in space and into each other for however long it takes us to tame our lust. When I come back to my senses, he carries me to the sofa, and for a brief moment he stands tall in front of me, towering over me with his nudity. Before I can take in all of the muscles in his chest, he's crowding me again in the most exalting way. A strange expression flashes across his face, and as his eyes lock into mine I have a sudden vision of a wounded animal crying for help. He comes closer, hugs me, holds me, and when I burry my face into his neck to nibble it, I can hear him murmur to my ear: "I've missed you."

And after that, nothing else matters.

EIGHTEEN

I think there really is an argument to be made for cold pizzas after sex.

We're sitting on the floor, leaning against his sofa, unabashedly savouring this homemade dinner that we've blissfully ignored for the past hour. My dress, discarded earlier, still lies forgotten in a crumpled heap in a corner of the room, and I can feel the still lightly damp skin in my back clinging to the leather cushions. Hugo is sitting right beside me, in his underwear, his left arm casually draped over the sofa, drawing me close to him.

I have wolfed down a copious amount of slightly wilted salad (the dressing *was* delicious) and three slices of lukewarm pizzas, and I'm now sipping my wine in silence, my heart and stomach content. I can't resist stealing glances at him, captivated by the glistening beads of sweat lingering on his forehead and just above the curve of his upper lip.

He must feel my eyes on him because he glances at me and I avert my gaze sheepishly, but I'm not quick enough and his lips curve into a smirk.

"I can't tell if you're staring at me or at my food."

"Definitely your food," I lie, even though the bloat in my stomach doesn't. I suddenly become hyper-aware of the rolls of my skin and I sit up straighter, casually resting my arm on my belly to hide the bump.

"There's dessert in the fridge," he adds, unaware of my self-conscious thoughts. "I hope it's had time to set."

I give him an intrigued look and he nudges me towards the open kitchen. I get on my feet and head to the fridge, trying not to think too much about the view I am offering him in doing so—but glad I followed Charlotte's advice on the choice of underwear.

"No, you didn't!" I gasp as I lay eyes on a large dish of chocolate mousse.

"There's sea salt in the cupboard above the oven," he says. I swiftly move around the space to grab spoons and a couple of bowls and return to my spot next to him. I scoop out large dollops of perfectly textured mousse into our bowls as he swallows his last bit of pizza, and then expertly sprinkle a finishing touch of sea salt on top.

"I can't promise it's as good as the one from Boro Bistro, but I hope you like it."

I shove a spoonful of mousse inside my mouth and let it melt on my tongue, sending my taste buds into a frenzy. "It's possibly the best thing I've ever eaten in my life," I say, all of my self-conscious thoughts vanished.

"Well, thanks, but I think I need to take you out more because trust me, there are many, many better things out there."

I shove another mouthful of mousse into my mouth so I don't have to comment on what he just said. Not the modesty part—the hinting at going out together again part. I know men sometimes talk about the future without really meaning it, and then they act all confused when we get into our heads and follow up on their empty promises—I've learned it the hard way with Elliott. But in the short time Hugo and I have been dating, I've done more than my share of overthinking already and it hasn't worked too well for us.

I put my spoon down and swallow the rest of my mousse, and then, keeping my tone as casual as I can, I ask him the question that's been playing on my mind for the past half hour.

"So… what was this? Goodbye sex?"

"I mean, I'm up for going again, just give me ten mi—"

"You know that's not what I mean."

"I know," he sighs, and he frowns as he turns to face me. "But I'm only going away for two weeks. You'll still be here when I'm back, right?"

"Yes, I will," I admit, "but it doesn't change that I'm moving away soon. And then what?"

"Well, you tell me."

I'm stunned to silence, not sure what to say. I wasn't expecting this. He drops his arm wrapped around me as he sits up straighter and shifts his torso so as to face me, his expression suddenly more serious.

"Ellie, I'm not the one walking away from you. Okay yes, maybe I did that day on the beach," he says. "But that was a mistake and I have no intention to make it again. For months, White Cuppa House was just a pit stop on my morning commute to work, I just came and went and that was it. Full disclosure, I wasn't even that loyal of a customer, and if I'm being completely honest I still think Maggy Mug makes better coffee."

"Excuse me?" I scoff. "Maggy Mug on Grange Road?"

"Yes. They source their coffee exclusively from Colombia and they use filtered water—but that's not the point," he says, his voice raising a bit as he sees I'm about to interrupt. "The point is, after you joined White Cuppa House, I couldn't have cared less if Maggy Mug won the best London coffee award, because you became the key ingredient to my morning coffee."

I remain completely silent, staring at him in disbelief, and this time resist the urge of pinching myself for the second time tonight.

"I still remember the first time I saw you," he adds with a weak smile. "It was a Wednesday in January, I was late for work and in a bit of a rush, and I remember I almost gave up when I realised how slowly the line was moving. But when I looked behind the counter to see what the hold-up was, I saw you. You were so focused on what Charlotte was showing you, with your cheeks all red and your hair coming off from your ponytail. You looked like you were trying so hard to take everything in and not panic under pressure. So I decided not to be a dick and rush you off, and I just waited for my turn and watched you prepare everyone else's drinks, and then mine."

"Did you arrive late at work?"

"Oh yes, massively. It's a good thing I'm good at my job and I can get away with getting to a meeting 10 minutes late. That, and the fact I'm a cis white man, I suppose. And for all my troubles that day, I didn't even get to look at you properly. When my turn came, you didn't even look at me when I told you what I wanted and you went straight to the machine to prepare my americano."

"Sorry."

"It's fine. I came back, didn't I?" he says looking at me with the most adorable smile. "From that day, I couldn't explain why but I felt drawn to you. You always looked so warm and kind, with your beautiful laugh, and I saw you get better and better at the job over the weeks and in a weird way I was feeling almost... proud? I just knew I wanted to get to know you better."

"What took you so long then?" I tease with a little jab to his ribs.

"A mix of things, to be honest. The main one being that White Cuppa House really is my morning stop on the way to work, and I didn't want to start up a conversation with you when I knew I'd have to rush out. I tried to stop by some afternoons when I was working from home, but you weren't there because I figured you only worked part time. So it wasn't easy to pin you down—and I didn't even know if you were single or remotely interested, so that didn't help. Honestly, Ellie, if you gave me signs, I didn't see them."

"I—no," I admit sheepishly, "I mean, *yes*, I was interested, of course!" I add when I see his face freeze and realise how it sounded.

"But I had no idea you were too, and I wasn't really thinking about dating anyway."

"Well, if you ask me, more people should be more open about their romantic interests and situation because that would save everyone a lot of time," he says and I can't help but chuckle. "So anyway, months passed and I still hadn't found a way to ask you out until the perfect opportunity came."

"The flat white gate?"

"The flat white gate. A blessing in disguise. And even then, I wasn't sure how it would go because you looked like you were in a pretty bad mood."

I cast my mind back to Raf's cappuccino and Cassandra's state of constant panic that morning. "I was having a rough shift," I concede.

"Right. So I must have been completely out of my mind to ask you out that day of all days, but you still said yes and then I couldn't wait for the Sunday to arrive. And…well, the rest is history," his voice trails off and for a brief moment, he breaks eye contact with me, as if he was realising how vulnerable he's been for the past few minutes.

But he must realise it's too late to go back now, because he continues, his tone serious and assured.

"The reason why I'm telling you all this, Ellie, is because I *know* what it looked like when I left you in Brighton and then didn't call you back. Especially knowing that you had doubts on whether I was seeing other people—it must have made the whole thing even worse. So yes, I know it looks bad, but I promise you, I hadn't given up on you. On us. I had waited *months* to ask you out and I hated that things got cut short on a misunderstanding, but I just thought…" He sighs, rubbing his face. "I thought we both needed a bit of time for things to settle down, but we'd find our way back to each other again. I hoped so, anyway."

He raises a hand to my cheek, brushing it softly, and leans forward, bringing his face so close to mine that I can feel his sweet breath tingling my lips.

"And now, we have. So if you think that I'm going to let a couple hundreds of miles and a few hours on the train break us apart again, think again. If you tell me this isn't what you want and it's too much stress, I'll respect that, Ellie. I'd understand. But you're going to have to say it and mean it, because I'm not going anywhere."

He looks at me with his sea-blue eyes, and suddenly I can't hold it any more. I close the gap between us and devour his lips and his words.

And my kiss means more than anything I could ever have said.

NINETEEN

"This is such a nice flat, Ellie!"

Lia has had this look of awe etched on her face since the moment she stepped into the flat half an hour ago. I've shown her every corner of every room and told her about all the little quirks (like the sink that was built the wrong way around and the loud fan in the bathroom), which she doesn't seem to mind one bit.

I still remember when I visited it for the first time, and how I projected myself through the boxes and suitcases of the previous tenants. And now, showing Lia around, I am torn between pride and nostalgia, and the bittersweet thoughts of handing over my beloved flat to someone else. Although, if it really must be this way, I couldn't imagine a better person for it.

I haven't known Lia for very long, but she's already won me over (as well as Amar, evidently). She's rather introverted and often stays quiet in group settings, but when you get to know her better, you soon realise how big both her heart and her brain are. She works as a nurse at Guy's Hospital and still lives with her parents and three younger sisters, but at twenty-seven she's starting to think about leaving the nest and fly with her own gorgeous wings. Good for her.

"I'm glad you like it," I say, meaning it. "And I'm sorry it's all still very much up in the air, but I promise I'll keep you posted as soon as I know more."

"Have you not heard anything back yet?"

"No, not yet. But I'm applying to other places and I have an interview on Monday with another company from Bolton, near Manchester, so hopefully something comes out of it."

And if I'm being honest, my motivation to look for a job two hundred miles from here is at an all-time low after my reunion with Hugo, but the butterflies and rosy-pink glasses can't do much to help my financial situation and I still need to get my life back on track. I just have to trust him and us to make it work from a distance.

"Well, I'll keep my fingers crossed for you," she says encouragingly, as if she could read my mind.

"Thanks." The flat is pretty warm from the accumulated heat of the day, and even though I have to credit my brand-new fan with a solid effort at bringing the temperature down, the breeze coming out from the open window is still far more refreshing. "Do you fancy a walk? You can ask me more questions if you like—but fair warning, I want to know everything about you and Amar in return."

***

When I walk through the doors of The Folly the following day, the pulsing energy you would expect from that kind of establishment on a Thursday night pulls me in like a friendly embrace. Conversations intertwine with bursts of laughter, and the clinking of glasses and cacophony of voices creating an irresistible energy.

Located near London Bridge, The Folly is a go-to destination for those working nine-to-five jobs in the city, making it the perfect choice for special occasions like hen dos, baby showers, and leaving drinks. The restaurant offers a versatile space, from cosy nooks adorned with plush cushions for intimate conversations to lively communal tables where strangers quickly become friends. Every corner of the restaurant is thoughtfully curated, boasting a blend of natural elements and urban chic. Lush foliage cascades from the ceiling, potted plants and hanging vines adorning the interior, as if these touches of nature could impart somewhat of a sense of tranquillity amidst the vibrant crowd.

It doesn't take me long to spot Debbie's table, by far the loudest one in the room, and I quickly make my way through the crowd of city dwellers to join in on the cheerful buzz of her friends and colleagues gathered to celebrate her.

"Ellie!" Debbie exclaims as she sees me.

Before I can do so much as present her with her birthday card and her gift, she engulfs me in an enthusiastic hug. She squeezes me so tight I can barely breathe—and the air that I do inhale is loaded with wafts of prosecco and espresso martinis that I can imagine have already been flowing freely before I arrived. I pat her on the arm, much like a defeated judoka tapping out, and she finally loosens her embrace.

Gosh, she is strong for a drunk person.

"I'm so glad you're here. You really were my favourite colleague ever."

"I've missed you too," I reply fondly. "Here, this is for you."

"Ooooh thank you so much!" she says before even laying eyes on what I got for her. "You're so, so sweet. Come here, let me introduce you—at least, to the people you don't know yet."

She grabs me by the arm and pulls me in her stride towards her group of friends. I recognise a few faces, including Chris from the accounting department and two women I've seen on Debbie's story, but mostly these are brand new faces. New, rather rosy in the cheek and particularly smiley faces—I'm guessing they all came here straight from work and have already had a few glasses each.

"Everyone, this is Ellie," she says to the group, and I hear a few "Hi Ellie" as I awkwardly wave at Debbie's friends. She turns back to me and, cupping her hand above her mouth in a childish way, she whispers, "There's someone I want to introduce you to." I raise my eyebrows at her, intrigued, and she peers around her until she seemingly spies that someone by the bar and beckons me to follow her.

"Ellie, this is Mark; Mark, this is Ellie."

Mark, who was leaning against the bar a second ago trying to get the staff's attention, peers up and grants me the most charming smile I have ever seen. His teeth are impeccably white, his face elegant and warm. He has perfectly well moisturised hands, no hair and no beard, and judging by the tiny wrinkles just settling in the corner of his eyes, I would place him in his late forties.

"Nice to meet you, Ellie. What are you drinking?"

"Oh no, don't worry, I'll get my own—"

"No, no, please, I insist. Debbie's been raving on about you and how stupid we've been to let you go with the merger, it's the least I can do."

I blush at the compliment, giving Debbie an *I can't believe you* look. "Well, then... A Gin&Tonic would be great. Thanks."

He nods and turns his back to us, trying once again to get the staff's attention. Debbie looks at me all giggly, and before I can ask her what's going on, she blurts out: "This is the guy I was telling you about. The hot guy from Vonders."

"The..." my mouth gapes open in understanding, and my eyes immediately go back to Mark's neck while Debbie still nods excitedly at her news.

"We've been dating since the party," she clarifies, completely unaware of the eureka moment that I'm still trying to process. I feel like I'm in a silly cartoon and a thousand light bulbs have just been switched on in my brain and are now blinking like Christmas lights.

I can't believe I've been so *stupid*.

"He's been great," she adds fondly. "He did swoon at my dress, but as it turns out, he likes me for my incredible wits and my brains, too."

"Of course he does! He'd be stupid not to," I reply, getting over my surprise.

"True. But what about you? How is it going with your guy?"

"Oh trust me, we both need a drink for that story," I reply, and as if on cue, Mark turns around with three large glasses of G&T, while Debbie lets out an excited "whoop!"

TWENTY

At first, I think it's my pounding headache that just jolted me awake, and for a few moments, I can't quite make sense of the world around me. But as I lie there in agony for ten solid mississippis, I realise my phone is buzzing next to my ear.

"Mother of—" I mumble, fumbling to find my phone, but by the time I locate it I'm too late and whoever had the *audacity* to call me so early has already hung up.

After I told Debbie the whole story yesterday, we both had a good laugh and a long overdue catch up on our dramas. As it turns out, Mark actually works quite closely with Hugo and I got some very juicy insider tips from him. The highlight was when his face suddenly lit up in comprehension as I recounted him and Debbie what happened in Brighton.

"So *that's* why he was off his game for the whole rest of the week!" he exclaimed, and I must admit, I felt pretty smug. After that, I let myself go to euphoria, relief and mixed alcohols, and while I am *sourly* regretting it today, it was a great night.

I think.

When my hands finally find my screen, I raise one eyelid just enough to see that it is 11:15 and that the missed call is from an unknown number. I groan, dropping my phone back on the mattress, but the next second my phone buzzes again, signalling a voice message. Half expecting a random note meant for someone else, I press play and let my head sink into the pillow again.

Not for long.

I recognise the subtle Geordie accent instantly. I spring to my feet—or at least sit up straight—and regret it immediately as my head starts throbbing as if it's been pummelled by a thousand golf balls. Still, I force myself to steady my wavering composure, pushing aside the loud thumping of my heart in my forehead to focus on Emma's voice.

"Hi Ellie, it's Emma from Mancunia Motion Pictures, Juliette gave me your phone number. I just sent you an email and I thought we could discuss it over the phone once you've had a chance to read it. I'm headed to the airport now so if you can call me back before 12:00 that'd be great; otherwise I'll hopefully speak to you on Monday."

I scramble up to my feet and scurry to the living room to find my laptop abandoned in the corner of the coffee table and slam it open as I drop into the sofa. A moment later, I open my mailbox, anticipation and adrenaline keeping my hangover temporarily at bay.

And here it is. At the top of my mailbox, the bold subject line signalling a new unread email reads: *Confidential—Offer Letter—Mancunia Motion Pictures x Ellie Matthews.*

I let out a triumphant shriek that vibrates as much through the room as it does in my head, and I hastily click the subject line to reveal the whole email.

Dear Ms Matthews,

We have the pleasure to inform you that, having been most impressed by your portfolio and your experience, we would like to offer you a position as Senior Motion Graphics Designer at Mancunia Motion Pictures.

Please find attached your offer letter. Kindly confirm that you are happy with the stated terms so we can prepare your contract.

We look forward to welcoming you as a permanent member of staff at Mancunia Motion Pictures.

Yours sincerely,

Emma McLane

COO Mancunia Motion Pictures

My heart does a wild dance in my chest as I read the email again and again, hardly able to believe the words on the screen.

I have a job. I actually have a job.

As I am still revelling in the news, my phone starts buzzing again and my throat tightens immediately as I see the name of the caller flashing on my screen.

Liam never calls me. *Ever.*

This can't be good.

"Hey giggle-saurus," he greets me as I pick up. It's been my nickname since I was six and he was four and he burst out laughing at my homemade costume of the queen of dinosaurs at his Jurassic Park themed birthday party. I was almost in tears when Dad intervened and called me a *giggle-saurus* and warned my little brother that I was the most dangerous of dinosaurs, and that he'd better watch out — you should have seen his face.

"Is everything okay?" I blurt out anxiously. "What happened?"

"Wh—well, hello to you too, so nice to speak to you. Have you not had your morning coffee yet? Why isn't your camera on?"

"Liam—"

"Turn on your camera!" I huff and do as I'm told. "Wow you look like shit."

"Thanks. That's why I didn't have my camera on," I grumble, flattening my hair with my spare hand although I'm acutely aware that my puffy eyes and the smooched make-up are the main reasons for my less-than-stellar appearance. However, I feel my shoulders relaxing at Liam's chipper voice and playful tone, because they mean that whatever he's calling about can't be that bad.

"Why are you calling me?"

"Because *we* have something to say," he replies as he pulls his phone away, revealing Orla in the frame.

"Hi Ellie!" Orla waves with a gleaming smile that's almost blinding.

A smile almost as shiny as the sparkly ring on her finger.

Oh my god.

"You're engaged!" I exclaim, my eyes welling up. That's a bit of a dramatic reaction, but what can I say—it's been an *intense* morning. "Oh my god, congratulations! I'm so happy for you! Show me the ring, Orla."

Orla brings her hand closer to the camera, giving me a close-up view of the beautiful ring on her finger—a golden band with serrated diamonds and a dazzling green emerald. As his only sister, of course, I am a bit offended that he didn't feel the need to consult me for the choice of the ring, but I have to admit, my brother has taste.

"It's beautiful," I say, still captivated by it.

"And that's not all," Liam interjects, clearly enjoying the dramatic build-up. "You're going to be an auntie!"

What?!" My jaw drops—this is too much for one morning. Thank God I'm already sitting down, or else I'd definitely faint and collapse on the spot. "Since when?! I mean—no, don't answer that," I add quickly as I see a smirk tugging at Liam's lips. "When are you due?"

"Mid-January. And before you ask, no, I didn't propose to Orla because she told me she was pregnant. This was a well thought through, *very romantic* proposal in the park where we took our first walk."

"I wasn't—why would anyone even think that? It's not the 1960s any more."

"Well, ask Uncle George. He's the one that made that comment."

"You told Uncle George before me?" I hiss, positively outraged.

Liam holds up his hands in defence. "Hey, don't shoot the messenger! It was Aunt Agnes's birthday, and you know how our family gatherings go. There's no hiding anything—especially not when Orla turns down cheese and wine."

I pout, the jealousy and FOMO swirling in my stomach like a tornado. Living far from family has its drawbacks, and missing out on juicy news is definitely one of them.

Well, not for much longer.

"I have something to share too," I announce cheerfully, and both of them peer up, intrigued. "I got a job! At Mancunia Motion Pictures— "I was just reading the offer letter when you interrupted me with your small, not at all life-changing news."

"Oh my god!" Liam gasps. "Ellie that's such good news! Wait, hold up… does that mean you're moving back for sure then? Mam said you were thinking about it."

"Yes, it looks like it. I'll have to sort it out and move back before the first day, I suppose. Sort myself out and all that."

Liam grins like a Cheshire cat, and I can see where this is going. "So, does that mean you'll be available for some babysitting duties?"

I nod, rolling my eyes playfully. "Yes, yes, you've got yourself a babysitter. But let's get one thing straight—I'm not changing diapers!"

"Sure, sure," Liam's voice trails off in a dismissive tone I don't like. "So when do you start?"

"I'm not sure—hang on let me have a look." I go back to the email to open the attachment and my eyes hover over the *generous* package and salary until they land on the desired starting date.

Oh.

"Ellie?"

"They want me to start on the 13th of July," I say, and Liam's eyes widen in shock.

"Crikey, that's soon. That's in…what, two weeks from now?"

"Yep."

"Well, better get packing then." Ever the practical one, my little brother.

I gulp, feeling like I've just been hit by a double-decker bus. My hangover is staging a comeback, and suddenly, I feel hot and shivery.

"I have to go, guys," I manage to squeak, attempting to flash a casual smile, even though I can see from the little square on the screen that I'm sporting a lovely shade of jaundice. "But congratulations, I'm so, so happy for you, and I can't wait to celebrate in person!"

"Thanks, Ellie, congrats to you too!" Orla chimes in cheerfully.

With a final little wave goodbye, I hastily cut the call, fearing that any minute now, I might turn into a human fountain. I race to the bathroom, my emotions from this morning and the drinks from last night doing a strange dance in my stomach.

Ugh, why can't I be twenty again? Of all the days to nurse a hangover, this has to be the worst timing ever, but does my body care? No, it does not.

After what feels like an eternity, I finally stop retching and manage to drag myself back to the living room. My phone tells me it's ten past twelve—technically not morning any more, but I try giving Emma a call back. It goes straight to voicemail. Great, just great.

Now what?

I fetch a large glass of water and retreat to the solace of my bed. Lying there with my eyes closed, I already feel a smidgen better and desperate for a nap, but my brain has other plans. It's decided to replay this morning's rollercoaster of emotions frame by frame.

I have a job—a smashing job with an excellent salary. Liam is getting married, and I'm going to be an aunt. I'm moving back to Manchester, back to my family.

I'm going to quit my job at the café and leave London. By the time Hugo returns from his holidays, I'll be gone.

My eyes snap open, and it's as if a thunderbolt has struck me.

By the time Hugo returns from his holidays, I'll be gone.

TWENTY-ONE

I bite my lips nervously as I wait for my call to go through.

"Hello?"

"Hi! How is it going?" I ask, trying my best to sound casual.

"Good," Hugo replies, sounding surprised but pleased by my call. "I'm just on my lunch break, finishing my packing and all that, so I can't stay too long. Everything okay?"

"Yes, yes, all good!" I reply in a high-pitched voice that probably won't fool him. "I was just thinking I could maybe pop by this afternoon before you go? To deliver an Americano and a kiss?"

"That sounds really nice, I'd love that. But I need to leave at 5:00, though, will that be okay?"

"Yes, that's fine. I'll see you later then!" I say and I hung up. My phone bleeps to signal a low battery—no wonder, after all the action it got this morning. I plug it into charge and decide it is time I pulled myself together and shake off this lethargic state. I have a million things to do and think about, but first, I need a bath.

***

Ah, the trusty sunglasses, ultimate disguise of red carpet stars and hungover baristas alike—protecting me from the sun and the world from my still puffy eyes. Today, they are an absolute necessity.

As I make my way to White Cuppa House, the June sun unleashes its final rays, turning my freshly washed skin into a sweaty mess. By the time I step into the café, a big under-boob sweat patch spruces up my pink cotton jumpsuit. Classy, Ellie, really classy.

"Hello, what can I get you?" Cassandra asks without recognising me.

"Ahem—an iced almond latte and a focaccia sandwich please. Is—is Charlotte around?"

"Oh, hi Ellie!" Cassandra says when she hears my voice. "Sorry, I didn't recognise you with those sunglasses. Yes, she's just in the kitchen, she won't be a minute."

"Thanks." I pay and stand aside, waiting patiently for my order and for my friend to return. A few moments later, the kitchen door swings open, and out comes a flushed Charlotte, balancing a tray of pastries and buns. My heart goes out to her—working in a hot kitchen on a scorching day is no joke.

"Hi, love," she beams when she spots me, and I have to resist the urge to don an apron and rush over to help her. "What brings you here?"

"That's a very good question, and I've got not one but three answers for you," I reply, feeling a bit dramatic.

"Oh dear, should I sit down for this?"

"Maybe. Hopefully not. But do you have ten minutes to spare? Thank you," I quickly add as Cassandra hands me my lifesaving drink and a toasty sandwich. Turning back to Charlotte, I continue, "That was answer number one."

"I'm taking ten with Ellie," Charlotte announces as she swiftly unties her apron. Cassandra doesn't seem to mind, barely sparing her a nod. "Let's go sit in the park and grab some air. It's boiling in here."

We saunter out of the café and take a turn around the corner, entering a cute little park adjacent to the bustling White Cuppa House. This pocket-sized oasis mainly serves as a shortcut connecting Bermondsey Street to Tower Bridge Road. Oh, and it's also a playground for local dog owners who bring their fur babies here for some much-needed exercise. The grass is so dry and yellow, it's like someone swapped it for hay. And the trees? Well, they're putting in minimal effort on the shade front at this time of day.

"It's like being in a giant oven," Charlotte exclaims, fanning herself with her petite hand like a lady in distress. I'm right there with her, taking refuge in my iced almond latte. "So, spill the beans. What's the big news?"

"Well… I got an email from Emma this morning. You know, Juliette's friend?"

"And…?"

"I got the job!" I say, barely managing to keep my coffee from becoming a casualty of Charlotte's enthusiastic lunge across the bench.

"Oh my god, Ellie, that's incredible! I'm so proud of you, so happy for you! About time someone realises they need you in their team. Well, someone other than me. Oh, but I'm so sad that means you have to leave though—what am I going to do without you?" she pouts.

"You'll be fine, you'll make friends with the next barista in less time than it takes Cassandra to make a chai latte," and she lets out a laugh (it's funny because it's true). "But… that's the second reason I needed to see you today. Charlotte Phoebe O'Callaghan, I am officially handing you my notice."

She gasps dramatically, clasping her hands over her mouth. "What, already?! But you're only on one-week notice…when are you starting the new gig?"

"In two weeks." Her eyes instantly widen in shock. "Which is why I needed to tell you today."

"What did Hugo say?"

I sigh. "And that's your third answer. I need you to prepare the very best Americano to go so that he can swallow the pill better when I tell him. And actually," I glance at my phone, "I should probably get going."

Charlotte sighs and pulls me into one more clammy hug, and we rise up to our feet to head back to White Cuppa House.

***

Half an hour later, I am standing outside Hugo's door, holding a scalding hot Americano in this blazing heat. Who on earth craves a hot coffee on a day like this? Well, Hugo apparently. I checked with him before I got it, and strongly hinted at how an iced coffee might be a better idea, but he didn't budge.

"Hey, you," he greets me with that perfect smile as he opens the door. A quick peck on the lips, and I'm invited in. "Thanks, you're a star," he says, gratefully grabbing the cup I'm offering him.

I wouldn't have thought of Hugo as a last-minute, disorganised packer, but judging by the state of his living room, this man is not ready to leave in two hours. A variety of rather damp clothes are hung out to dry on the rack, and it looks like he's scattered little piles of stuff everywhere with the intention, I presume, to eventually move them into the empty suitcase lying wide open in the middle of the room, begging to be filled.

Hugo himself isn't looking too put together either, with his hair dishevelled and his face revealing the stress of last-minute packing. But the moment he spots me, he tries to brush it off and be all smooth.

He takes a gulp of coffee (how is he not burning his tongue off?!), places the cup on the kitchen counter, and pulls me into a bear hug. For a moment, we both soak in each other's calming presence, the world fading away.

As we release from our embrace, he tilts my chin up, his eyes scanning my face. "How are you? You look a bit tired," he says, concern lacing his voice.

"I'm alright, didn't get much sleep. Debbie's thing went on forever," I reply.

"Things are all good between the two of you, then?"

"Yes," I say with a weak smile. "I even met your colleague Mark from finances. They've been dating since the launch party. Yes, I know, I know," I add sheepishly as I can see he's about to make a smug comment.

"Well, I'm glad you had fun," he says nonchalantly, his lips curling in a smile. "And I'm glad you're here. It's a nice surprise."

"Hold that thought because I have something to tell you."

He frowns and takes a step back, leaning against the counter, his eyes locked into mine. "That sounds serious."

Oh boy, hold on to your coffee cup, because here comes the moment of truth.

I take a deep breath, trying to maintain eye contact, but it's like staring at a beautiful, captivating, and slightly intimidating painting. "It kind of is. I mean, nothing *too* serious, but…" my voice falters and I have to look away. I've been psyching myself up for this conversation the whole morning, but now that I'm about to say it out loud, my throat is tight.

"Ellie, what is it?" He nudges me, and his tone is so soft that my eyes well up a little, my cheeks instantly flushing.

"I got a job in Manchester, and I'm starting in two weeks."

There. I said it. The cat is out of the bag, and I'm bracing myself for the backlash. Which is why I am *very confused* to see his eyes light up, and a grin spread across his face, a split second before he wraps his arms around my waist, lifting me from the floor and swirling me (and the focaccia sandwich in my stomach) around.

"Oh my god, congratulations! I'm so happy for you."

When he finally puts me back down, my face must look like a puzzle with missing pieces. Here I was, ready for an emotional showdown, and instead, I'm getting swept off my feet (literally) in a congratulatory dance. Is this man for real?

Hugo must notice my baffled look because he asks: "What? Is that not good news? I thought that's what you wanted."

"Did you hear the part where I start in two weeks?"

"Yes?"

"And…you're cool with that? You don't you have questions? Concerns? A moment of hesitation? Panic attack, perhaps?"

He frowns. "Do I have a choice?"

"What do you mean?" I ask, bemused.

"Well, what's the alternative? If you're asking me how I feel about you leaving London so soon, of course, I'm not thrilled. It's not ideal for us—not for me, anyway, because I like having you around. I like taking you out for dinner, and I wish I could have surprised you with breakfast in bed. I wish I hadn't waited so long to ask you out in the first place. I wish we'd had more time together. But it'd be foolish of me to think that you'd be content just settling with me in London and that you would stop chasing your dreams because of a guy. I know you're driven, you're talented, and you're smart, and these are all the reasons why I fell for you in the first place. I wouldn't expect you to turn own a fantastic career opportunity for my sake. Actually, I would be pretty mad at you if you did."

He stops briefly to catch his breath, and I remain perfectly quiet, too stunned to speak. Did he just say he fell for me? Like, really fell? Cue the melting heart.

"I don't want you to ever stop pursuing your career, wherever it may take you, because I want you to be happy," he continues, "and I know you can be happy without me, but you can't be happy without a purpose and a job you love. And that doesn't even bruise my ego, because that's exactly how I want the person I share my life with to be. I want you to succeed in what you love, and I want to be there for you, cheering you on from the sidelines, just like I want you to be there for me. But the mindset matters so much more than the distance, and I genuinely believe we can make it work."

He extends his arms in front of him to grab my hands and pulls me gently towards him. "I'm going to miss seeing your face in the morning at the café," he says softly, "I'm going to miss *you* like crazy. But I know it's for the best, and I'll make sure I take a mental picture of it every time I visit you in Manchester to remind myself every day how lucky I am to have found you in time."

Swoon alert! Has it got even hotter in here or is it just me? "Jeez, Hugo," I say, feeling all fuzzy and warm. "That's—"

"Too much? Sorry. But look, Ellie… I think both you and I have had disappointments in the past, and I would hate for you to freak out again because you don't know where this is going. So there you have it. I'm here if you'll have me. I know what I want. And I know I haven't always done the right thing in the past, and I'm not saying this will be easy, but we just have to take it one day at a time and remind ourselves why we're doing this. We'll figure it out."

I smile at him, my heart full, my lips burning with three silly little words that I know I won't say today, that I will keep locked away a little longer, but that are igniting a fire within me that Hugo's sea-blue eyes do nothing to tame.

I lean into him, surrendering to the feeling of contentment and security washing over me. Because he's right. We can make this work, even if it's not exactly how I imagined it.

I pull away from him and search his eyes, finding them fondly looking down on me, with a hint of apprehension I hurry to shake away.

"Fine. You win, Romeo. We're doing this. But I do have one more question for you."

"What's that?"

I flash him a cheeky grin. "How can someone be so reasonable and romantic, and at the same time, be so terrible at packing?"

TWENTY-TWO

The weekend is *dragging*.

It is Saturday afternoon, and the temperatures are yet again so absurdly high that the scent of melting asphalt is permeating through my windows. Obviously, in such a scorching heat, we've all agreed to call off the volleyball game. But being cooped up indoors has left me with no valid excuse to avoid the dreaded task of organising my move, and that nagging guilt is relentless. So here I am, sprawled on my sofa, gazing at the ceiling, trying to summon the motivation I sorely lack.

After our deep, heartfelt conversation yesterday—and admittedly a quick, more physical exchange as well—I reluctantly had to leave Hugo to his packing. It wasn't easy, especially when I don't know when we'll be able to meet up again, but after his Hugh Grant-worthy declaration leaving me all swoony and wobbly-kneed, I wasn't about to be the reason he missed his flight to Ireland. So I dragged myself back home and tried to tackle the daunting to-do list awaiting me.

It is safe to say that the last twenty-four hours have seen minimal progress, and my trusty thirty-minute-timer method has shamefully let me down. Never before have I been hit by such a severe case of procrastination. And I know the excitement for this new life will grow, I know it will. But still, the initial shock is... overwhelming. I mean, less than two weeks to uproot my entire London life and relocate to my childhood bedroom, with a job I can't even remember how to do? I can think of a few less stressful ways to spend the beginning of July.

I glance at my phone, reviewing the items on my to-do list, desperately seeking something I can tick off without lifting a finger. Cardboard boxes—ordered and arriving on Tuesday—tick. Plants—sorted to be rehomed at Charlotte's, with a slim chance of long-term survival—tick. I haven't yet told my landlady (or Lia) because I'm waiting to sign the contract first—half-tick. I have, however, told my parents, and they were so over the moon for me that I felt a twinge of guilt for my lack of excitement in comparison. I also tried reaching Emma again but my call went straight to voicemail, so I sent her an apologetic email, thanking her for the offer and promising to call her back first thing on Monday.

And then, I need to figure out what to do with the podcast. That's a big one, and honestly, I'm lost at sea, not knowing how to tackle it. *Ellie's Track* has been the heartbeat of my London life for the past few years, connecting me with incredible women and even leading me to my dream job. I owe it so much, and the idea of turning off the microphones for good and saying my goodbyes feels almost like a break-up with a long-time love. But it just wouldn't be the same in Manchester. I keep going back and forth with the question, debating what to do.I can hear Charlotte's words still resonating in my brain: "Record one final episode, Ellie," she suggested, "a last hurrah, all by yourself". At first, I brushed it off, of course. Thinking about all the incredible women I've met and the stories they've shared, I can't help but feel like my personal life story pales in comparison. But I have to admit. The idea is growing on me now. If I'm closing this chapter, I have to do it properly and bid farewell to *Ellie's Track* with grace and gratitude. Every life path is different, and each experience is valid. And every twist and turn has moulded me into who I am today and led me to this very moment, a delicate balance in my life where all the pieces have finally come together. And even if I'm feeling overwhelmed by the impending changes, I know that I'm exactly where I'm supposed to be.

***

When Monday finally arrives, I find myself wide awake long before seven, the morning sun stretching its warm fingers through my windows. After lying in bed for what feels like an eternity, I finally decide to get up and keep myself busy to shake off the restlessness. A stroll along the Thames seems like the perfect way to kill time before it becomes socially acceptable to ring up Emma.

I walk to Tower Bridge and decide to head east, walking through Shad Thames, and then close to the water again, soaking up the view and the atmosphere. When I reach Southwark Park, memories of our volleyball games flood my mind, and I feel a pang in my stomach when I realise I might never join in on them again if next week's session falls through too. It's one of these things that you used to take for granted and you don't notice them any more as they slip away quietly, until one day, you do them for the last time, without knowing it.

I get home just before nine and take a quick shower before sitting down behind my laptop and opening up Emma's email again. My heart starts racing in excitement as I dial her number.

It's getting real.

"Hello?" Emma's cheerful voice greets me on the other end of the line.

"Hi, it's Ellie Matthews."

"Oh, hi Ellie! How are you? Had a good weekend?"

"I did, thanks. Sorry I missed your call on Friday. But I did get your email and the offer, and—"

"No problem at all. I just wanted to make sure you're happy with the terms, especially the starting date. It's quite soon, but we have a new project kicking off on the 15th of July, and I'd really like you to take the lead on it. Hopefully, that won't be a problem?"

"No, not at all," I say hastily. "I can start on the 13th."

"Brilliant. Someone from HR will be in touch soon to confirm your address for equipment delivery."

My excitement wavers as I realise the logistics of setting up a chunky workstation in my tiny childhood bedroom. "Actually, I haven't found my permanent address in Manchester yet."

"Oh, I hadn't realised you were moving," Emma replies, sounding surprised. "How's the flat search going?"

Guilt settles in, making me feel like a schoolgirl caught skipping class. "I haven't properly started looking yet," I confess. "It's not easy from London, and there are a few things I need to sort out first. So I'll head back to my family home first, settle into the job, and then search for my permanent place. But until that's all sorted, I don't mind commuting to the office every day and using the workstations there. Would that be alright?"

A hushed pause follows, and then Emma asks, "I'm sorry, what do you mean?"

My cheeks burn with embarrassment, and I stumble over my words. "I meant I could use the office equipment temporarily until I'm settled and have the appropriate space for a workstation at home." The silence on the other end feels like a thousand eyes staring at me. "But if that's too much trouble, I'll figure something else out—"

Emma interrupts gently, "We don't have offices any more. Since the pandemic hit, we've fully embraced remote work. We gave up our lease and provided bonuses to our employees. A few of us are still based in Manchester, and the filming crew manages their travel arrangements for shoots, but most of our team has relocated, and some are even working from different time zones. So…there's no office for you to work from, I'm afraid."

Now it's my turn to fall silent while my mind tries to grasp this new piece of information and its implications. How did I miss that Mancunia Motion Pictures had shifted to a fully remote setup? I should have realised it when there was no mention of a specific location for my job. It's embarrassing, really.

"That's…fine," I falter, still processing this umpteenth plot twist.

"I'm sorry if there was any confusion," Emma adds, her voice bringing me back to Earth. "I hope this won't be too much of an issue? I hadn't realised you were planning on leaving London, you seemed to love it there when we met."

"I do. I— "I stutter, still in disbelief at the turn things are taking. "I love it here. I just..." My voice falters again, unable to cope with the flood of thoughts crashing and colliding in my brain.

Emma clears her voice. "Well, obviously, you must have your reasons for moving back up north, and I won't pry. I hope you find a nice place quickly. But please let us know where you'd like us to send your equipment and confirm your bank details. Raheem will guide you through all of this when he sends you the contract."

I try to steady my racing heart and maintain a professional tone in spite of the strange feeling of euphoria bubbling inside me. "Of course, I will."

"Great. I have to jump on another call, but it was good to speak to you. Let me know if you have any more questions and please keep me in copy of your exchanges with Raheem until the 13th."

I get up to my feet, unable to sit still any longer, adrenaline shooting pins and needles through my legs, my breath erratic. "No problem."

"Perfect. Oh and Ellie?"

"Yes?"

"Welcome to *Mancunia Motion Pictures*."

EPILOGUE

Six months later

My eyesight isn't what it used to be at the ripe age of thirty-three, but I'd recognise that tousled hair anywhere. And anyway, the moment Hugo steps outside the train at Manchester Piccadilly, it's almost as if I feel his presence close to me before I even lay eyes on his beautiful face.

"Hello, you," he greets me with a bright smile, wrapping his arm around me as he tugs along his little suitcase with the other.

"FInally," I sigh, nestling my head into the collar of his winter jacket, taking in his familiar scent. I could stay like this forever, although I wouldn't mind fewer layers of clothes between us. And also, we're supposed to meet my family for lunch, so I suppose we'd better get going and keep our clothes on—for now.

"Come on, let's go."

"Nice one," he remarks with an impressed whistle, eyeing the sleek, midnight-blue luxury sedan I just unlocked.

"Dad's special treat," I reply. "He let me borrow it with the condition that I always drive 10 mph below the speed limit. Don't ask me why; he doesn't follow that rule himself. What?" I enquire as Hugo smirks.

"Nothing."

"You know women can drive just as well as men, Hugo."

"Absolutely, and I never doubted *that*. But I also know *you*."

"If you're talking about that one time in Portugal, that was—"

"Shall we hit the road then? If you have to stick to the Ellie speed limit, we'd better get going. I wouldn't want to make a bad impression by arriving late for lunch."

He's got a point, I suppose. But even with my extra cautious driving, the journey from the station to my parents' home is a quick thirty minutes.

"Make sure you tell your dad I made you obey his rule," Hugo says as I pull up outside the family house. Mam appears at the front door as we step out and she beams gleefully as Hugo presents her the flowers he insisted we pick up on our way. Dad pulls me in a quick hug and gives Hugo a friendly pat on the back, and we follow him inside.

The table is already set with six plates (Dad will pick up Nan later for dessert), and Liam and Orla are comfortably seated on the sofa,

Liam's hand lovingly resting on her prominent belly. He rises from his seat as we arrive and Hugo extends his arm to greet him, and then bends down awkwardly to give Orla a kiss on each cheek.

"I still can't believe you're having twins!" I say, my eyes wide with amazement like every time I look at her beautiful baby bump. "I don't think I'll believe it even when they're here, to be honest."

"I know, it's quite the journey," Orla says with a laugh. "We'll definitely need a good babysitter."

"Come on everyone, let's eat before it gets cold," Mam calls, and I help Orla to her feet and support her arm as she wobbles to her chair. I take my place beside her and Hugo sits down to my right.

"Great choice on the bottle of wine, by the way," Dad compliments him from across the table. "It'll pair wonderfully with the pork."

Hugo smiles warmly, and I exchange a knowing glance with Dad, silently conveying my appreciation for his acceptance of Hugo into our family. It's been six months since we started dating, and having him here for the holidays feels like a beautiful step forward. I couldn't be happier.

As we pass the dishes around the table, conversation flows naturally, and just as I expected, his easy charm and relaxed demeanour win over everyone. I glance at my family and the man I love (we both said it on our little trip to Porto in September for my birthday and it was absolutely perfect) and as well of warmth fills my heart.

"I missed you," I whisper into Hugo's ear as the conversations flow around us.

"It's only been a week, babe," he replies with a little chuckle, his voice warm and affectionate, and places a gentle kiss on the corner of my lips.

"I know," I admit, "but it's the longest we've been apart since last summer, I'm not used to not seeing you every day any more."

He laughs, playfully nudging me. "That's true. But imagine if you actually had moved back here…how would you have coped?"

I respond with a little jab in the ribs, pretending to take offence. "Ha ha. I would have managed, thank you very much. In case you've already forgotten, I wasn't the one practically *begging* you to give us another chance when you found out I was moving away."

"*Touché*," he concedes, placing a generous portion of potatoes on my plate. "I did do that, didn't I?" He looks up at me with his usual adorable smile. "I'm glad I was convincing."

"You were."

"And I'm glad you stayed."

"Good."

I glance around at Mam, Dad, Liam and Orla. They were all a bit disappointed when I backtracked on my plans to move back, but also very understanding and supportive of my decision. And as a compromise, I've been making an effort to visit more often, and each time they would ask me when they'd finally get to meet the man that I chose over them.

I mean, it wasn't exactly like that. But…. Yes, admittedly, my 2.0 life in London with Hugo and the new job has been pretty amazing. No regrets.

"And I've missed you too," he finally admits and I beam at him with a triumphant smile. "Oh and Charlotte says hi."

After I left White Cuppa House, Charlotte and I have remained inseparable, and we rarely go a day without seeing, texting, or calling each other. I still often stop by the café, not just because it's undeniably the best in town (Hugo promised to remain loyal to White Cuppa House from now on and I've forgiven him for his brief lapse in judgment), but also because a part of me misses the time I spent working there with her.

Don't get me wrong, I love my new job. The first couple of months were intense, and I grappled with the imposter syndrome since the moment I was onboarded on the new project Emma had mentioned. But it's been five months now, and everything is going swimmingly. The client is pleased, and I'm learning new things every day. I had my first review with my line manager Sophia just before the Christmas break, and she hinted at a possible promotion for me next year.

As Hugo's hand brushes gently against my leg under the table, I soak in the moment, cherishing this perfect day. After the rollercoaster of a year I've had, there are times when I still can't quite believe my luck and how my life took such a turn for the best.

How did I get so lucky? How did I become the girl who has it all in the end?

Maybe that's what happens when you follow your heart and keep chasing your dreams.

You end up with a full cup.

Cheers!

THE END

Printed in France by Amazon
Brétigny-sur-Orge, FR